The Cat Who Played Post Office

Lilian Jackson Braun

First published in 1996 by Headline Book Publishing

Compass Press Large Print Book Series; an imprint of
ISIS Publishing Ltd, Great Britain, and Bolinda Press, Australia

Published in Large Print 1997 by ISIS Publishing Ltd,
7 Centremead, Osney Mead, Oxford OX2 0ES,
and Australian Large Print, Audio and Video Pty Ltd
17 Mohr Street, Tullamarine, Victoria 3043
by arrangement with Headline Book Publishing

British Library Cataloguing in Publication Data
Braun, Lilian Jackson
The cat who played post office.
– Large print ed. – (A Jim Qwilleran feline whodunnit)
1. American fiction – 20th century
2. Large type books
I. Title
813.5'4 [F]

National Library of Australia Cataloguing in Publication Data
Braun, Lilian Jackson
The cat who played post office/
Lilian Jackson Braun
l v. (large print). Cm.
ISBN 1863407022
1. Title

ISBN 0-7531-5510-9 (ISIS Publishing Ltd)
ISBN 1-86340-702-2 (ALPAV Pty Ltd)

Printed and bound by Hartnolls Ltd, Bodmin, Cornwall

CHAPTER ONE

A Caucasian male — fiftyish, six-feet-two, weight two-thirty, graying hair, bushy moustache — opened his eyes and found himself in a strange bed in a strange room. He lay still, in a state of peculiar lassitude, and allowed his eyes to rove about the room with mild curiosity. Eyes that might be described as mournful surveyed the steel footboard of the bed, the bare window, the hideous color of the walls, the television on a high shelf. Beyond the window a tree was waving its branches wildly.

He could almost hear his mother's musical voice saying, "The tree is waving to you, Jamesy. Wave your hand like a polite little boy."

Jamesy? Is that my name? It doesn't sound — exactly — right . . . Where am I? What is my name?

The questions drifted across his consciousness without arousing anxiety — only a vague perplexity.

He had a mental picture of an old man with a Santa Claus beard standing at his bedside and saying, "You haff scarlet fever, Jamesy. Ve take you to the hospital and make you vell."

Hospital? Is this a hospital? Do I have scarlet fever?

Although undisturbed by his predicament, he was

beginning to have an uncomfortable feeling that he had neglected something of vital importance; he had failed someone close to him. His mother, perhaps? He frowned, and the wrinkling of his brow produced a slight hurt. He raised his left hand and found a bandage on his forehead. Quickly he checked other parts of his anatomy. Nothing was missing and nothing seemed to be broken, but the movement of his right knee and right elbow was restricted by more bandages. There was also something unusual about his left hand. He counted four fingers and a thumb, and yet something was wrong. It was baffling. He sighed deeply and wondered what it could possibly be that he had neglected to do.

A strange woman — plump, white haired, smiling — bustled into the room with noiseless steps. "Oh, you're awake! You had a good night's sleep. It's a beautiful day, but windy. How do you feel, Mr Cue?"

Cue? Jamesy Cue? Is that my name?

It sounded unlikely, if not absurd. He passed his hand over his face experimentally, feeling a familiar moustache and a jaw he had shaved ten thousand times. As a voice test he said aloud to himself, "I remember the face but not the name."

"My name? Toodle," the woman said pleasantly. "Mrs Toodle. Is there anything I can do for you, Mr Cue? Dr Goodwinter will be here in a few minutes. I'll take your jug and bring you some fresh water. Are you ready for brekky?" As she left the room with the jug in hand, she called over her shoulder, "You have bathroom privileges."

Bathroom privileges. Brekky. Toodle.

They were foreign words that made no sense. The old man with a beard had told him he had scarlet fever. Now this woman was telling him he had bathroom privileges. It sounded like some kind of embarrassing disease. He heaved another sigh and closed his eyes to wait for the old man with a Santa Claus beard. When he opened them again, a young woman in a white coat was standing at his bedside, holding his wrist.

"Good morning, lover," she said. "How do you feel?"

The voice had a familiar ring, and he remembered her green eyes and long eyelashes. Around her neck hung a tubular thing, the name of which escaped him. Hesitantly he asked, "Are you my doctor?"

"Yes, and more — much more," she said with a wink.

He began to feel familiar sensations. *Is she my wife? Am I a married man? Am I neglecting my family?* Again he felt a twinge of guilt about the responsibility he was shirking, whatever it might be. "Are you — are you my wife?" he asked in a faltering voice.

"Not yet, but I'm working on it." She kissed an unbandaged spot on his forehead. "You still feel groggy, don't you? But you'll be A-OK soon."

He looked at his left hand. "Something's missing here."

"Your watch and ring are in the hospital safe until you're ready to go home," she explained gently.

"Oh, I see . . . Why am I here?" he asked fearfully, worrying about the indelicate nature of his disease.

"You fell off your bicycle on Ittibittiwassee Road. Do you remember?"

Ittibittiwassee. Bathroom privileges. Brekky. Groggy. What language, he wondered, were these people speaking? He ventured to ask, "Do I have a bicycle?"

"You *did* have a bike, lover, but it's totaled. You'll have to buy a ten-speed now."

Totaled. Ten-speed. Toodle. He shook his head in dismay. Clearing his throat, he said, "That woman who came in here said I have bathroom privileges. What is that? Is it — is it some kind of —"

"It means you can get out of bed and walk to the bathroom," said the doctor with a smile twitching her lips. "I'll be back when I've finished my rounds." She kissed him again. "Arch Riker is coming to see you. He's flying up from Down Below." Then she walked from the room with a long leggy stride and a chummy wave of the hand.

Arch Riker. Down Below. What was she talking about? And who was she? To ask her name would have been embarrassing under the circumstances. He shrugged in defeat, hoisted himself out of bed, and hobbled to the bathroom. There in the mirror were sad eyes, graying temples and an oversized pepper-and-salt moustache that he recognized. Still, the name eluded him.

When the woman who called herself Toodle brought a tray of what she called brekky, he ate the blob of something soft and yellow, the two brown patties that were salty and chewy, the triangular slabs of something thin and crisp, which he smeared with something red and sweet. But he was glad to lie down again and close his eyes and stop trying to think.

He opened them suddenly. A man was standing at his bedside — a paunchy man with thinning hair and a ruddy face that he had seen many times before.

"You dirty bird!" the visitor said genially. "You gave us a scare! What were you trying to do? Kill yourself? How do you feel, Qwill?"

"Is that my name? I can't remember."

The man gulped twice and turned pale. "All your friends call you Qwill. Short for Qwilleran. Jim Qwilleran, spelled with a *Q-w*."

The patient studied the information and nodded slowly.

"Don't you remember me, Qwill? I'm Arch Riker, your old sidekick."

Qwilleran stared at him. *Sidekick*. Another baffling word.

"We grew up together in Chicago, Qwill. For the last few years I've been your editor at the *Daily Fluxion*. We've had a million lunches at the Press Club."

The light began to penetrate Qwilleran's foggy mind. "Wait a minute. I want to sit up."

Riker pressed a button that raised the head of the bed and pulled up a straight chair for himself. "Melinda called me and said you fell off your bike. I came right away."

"Melinda?"

"Melinda Goodwinter. Your latest girl, Qwill. Also your doctor, you lucky dog."

"What is this place?" Qwilleran asked. "I don't know where I am."

"This is the Pickax Hospital. They brought you here after your accident."

"Pickax? What kind of a hospital is that?"

"Pickax City — four hundred miles north of everywhere. You've been living here for the last couple of months."

"Oh . . . Is that when I left Chicago?"

"Qwill, you haven't lived in Chicago for twenty years," Riker said quietly. "You've lived in New York, Washington — all around the country since then."

"Wait a minute. I want to sit in that big chair."

Riker picked up a red plaid bathrobe with ragged edges. "Here, get into this. It looks like yours. It's the Mackintosh tartan. Does that ring a bell? Your mother was a Mackintosh."

Qwilleran's face brightened. "That's right! Where is she? Is she all right?"

Riker drew a deep breath. "She died when you were in college, Qwill." He paused to formulate a plan. "Look here, let's go back to the beginning. I've known you ever since kindergarten. Your mother called you Jamesy. We called you Snoopy. Do you remember why?"

Qwilleran shook his head.

"You were always snooping into other kids' lunch boxes." He searched Qwilleran's face for a glimmer of recollection. "Do you remember our first-grade teacher? She was thin at the top and fat at the bottom. You said, 'Old Miss Blair looks like a pear.' Remember that?"

There was a slight nod and half smile in response.

"You were always good with words. You were playing with words when the rest of us were playing with water pistols." With patience Riker went on with the nostalgic recital, hitting the highlights of his friend's life. "You were spelling champ for three years . . . In junior high school you discovered girls . . . In high school you played baseball — outfield, good slugger. And you edited the school paper."

"*The North Wind*," Qwilleran murmured.

"That's it! That's the name! . . . After graduation you went into the service and came out with a trick knee, so that was the end of baseball. In college you sang in the glee club and got interested in acting." The years rolled by in a matter of minutes. "We both went into journalism, but you got the glamour assignments. You were tops as a crime reporter, and whenever there was any trouble overseas, they sent you to cover the hot spots."

With each revelation Qwilleran's mind became sharper, and he responded with more awareness.

"You won journalism prizes and wrote a book on urban crime. It actually got on the best-seller list."

"For about ten minutes."

Relief showed in Riker's face. His friend was beginning to sound normal. "You were my best man when I married Rosie."

"It rained all day. I remember the wet confetti."

"You were in Scotland when you married Miriam."

Again Qwilleran felt the vague uneasiness. "Where is she? Why isn't she here?"

"You were divorced about ten years ago. She's somewhere in Connecticut."

The mournful eyes gazed into space. "And after that everything fell apart."

"Okay, let's face it, Qwill. You developed a drinking problem and couldn't hold a job, but you snapped out of it and came to work for the *Daily Fluxion*, writing features. You turned out some good stuff. You could write about art, antiques, interior design — anything."

"Even if I didn't know anything about it," Qwilleran put in.

"When you started writing restaurant reviews, you could make food sound as interesting as crime."

"Wait a minute, Arch! How long have I been away from my desk? I've got to get back to work!"

"Hey, man, you quit several weeks ago!"

"What! Why did I quit? I need the job!"

"Not anymore, my friend. You inherited money — a bundle of it — the Klingenschoen fortune."

"I don't believe it! What am I doing? Where do I live?"

"Here in Pickax City. Those were the terms of the will. You have to live in Moose County for five years. You inherited a big house in Pickax with a four-car garage and a limousine and —"

Qwilleran grabbed the arms of his chair. "The cats! Where are the cats? I haven't fed the cats!" *That* was the thing that had been troubling the edges of his mind. "I've got to get out of here!"

"Don't get excited. You'll split your stitches. The brats are okay. Your housekeeper is feeding them, and she's making up a room for me so I can stay overnight."

"Housekeeper?"

"Mrs Cobb. I wouldn't mind going there right now

for a little shut-eye. I've been up since four o'clock this morning."

"I'll go with you. Where are my clothes?"

"Sit down, sit down, Qwill. Melinda wants to run a few tests. I'll check back with you later."

"Arch, no one but you could have dredged up all that ancient history."

Riker grabbed his friend's hand. "Are you feeling like yourself now?"

"I think so. Don't worry."

"See you later, Qwill. God! I'm glad to see you functioning again. You gave me a bad scare."

After Riker had left, Qwilleran tested himself. *Sidekick, shut-eye, brekky*. Now he knew the meaning of all the words. He could remember his own telephone number. He could spell *onomatopoeia*. He knew the names of his cats: Koko and Yum Yum, a pair of beautiful but tyrannical Siamese.

Yet, there was a period of a few hours that remained a blank. No matter how intensely he concentrated, he could not recall anything immediately before or immediately after the accident. Why did he fall off his bike? Did he hit a pothole or some loose gravel? Or did he pass out while pedaling? Perhaps that was Melinda's reason for wanting to run tests.

He was too tired to concentrate further. Recollecting his entire past had been an exhausting chore. In a single morning he had relived more than forty years. He needed a nap. He needed some *shut-eye*. Smiling to himself because he now knew all the words, he fell asleep.

Qwilleran slept soundly, and he had a vivid dream.

He was having lunch in a sunny room, all yellow and green. The housekeeper was serving macaroni-and-cheese flecked with green pepper and red pimiento. He could picture everything distinctly: the brown casserole, the housekeeper's bright pink sweater. In the dream the colors were so vibrant they were disturbing.

Qwilleran was telling Mrs Cobb that he might take a bike ride on Ittibittiwassee Road.

"Be careful with that rusty old crate," she said in a cheerful voice. "You really ought to buy a ten-speed, Mr Q . . . a ten-speed, Mr Q . . . a ten-speed, Mr Q . . ."

Suddenly he was awake; his bandaged brow was cold and wet. The sequence had been so real, he refused to believe it was a dream. There was only one way to be sure.

He reached for the telephone and dialed his home number, and when he heard his housekeeper's cheery hello he marveled at the audio-fidelity of his dream. "Mrs Cobb, how's everything at the house? How are the cats?"

"Oh, it's *you*, Mr Q," she squealed. "Thank goodness you're all in one piece! The cats? They miss you. Koko won't eat, and Yum Yum cries a lot. They know something's wrong. Mr Riker is here, and I sent him upstairs to take a nap. Is there anything you want, Mr Q? Anything I can send you?"

"No, thanks. Not a thing. I'll be home tomorrow. But just answer a couple of questions, if you will. Did you serve macaroni-and-cheese yesterday?"

"Oh Lord! I hope it wasn't the lunch that caused your spill."

"Don't worry. Nothing like that. I'm just trying to recall something. Were you wearing a pink sweater yesterday?"

"Yes, the one you gave me."

"Did I discuss my plans for the afternoon?"

"Oh, Mr Q! This sounds like one of your investigations. Do you have some suspicions?"

"No, just curious, Mrs Cobb."

"Well, let me think . . . You said you were going to take the old bike out for a ride, and I said you ought to buy a new ten-speed. You'll have to buy one now, Mr Q. The sheriff found your old one in a ditch, and it's a wreck!"

"In a ditch?" That's strange, Qwilleran thought, stroking his moustache thoughtfully. He thanked the housekeeper and suggested some delicacies to tempt Koko's appetite. "Where is he, Mrs Cobb? Put him on the phone."

"He's on top of the refrigerator," she said. "He's listening to every word I say. Let me see if the phone cord will reach."

There was an interlude in which Mrs Cobb could be heard making coaxing noises, while Koko's familiar yowl came through with piercing clarity. Then Qwilleran heard a snuffling sound coming from the receiver.

"Hello there, Koko old boy," he said. "Are you taking care of Yum Yum? Are you keeping the house safe from lions and tigers?"

A throaty purr came over the line. Koko appreciated intelligent conversation.

"Be a good cat and eat your food. You've got to keep up your strength to fight off all those jaguars and black buffalos. So long, Koko. I'll be home tomorrow."

"YOW!" came a sharp cry that stabbed Qwilleran's eardrum.

He replaced the receiver and turned to find Mrs Toodle standing there in wide-eyed astonishment. Her voice was wary. "I came to see . . . if you'd like to have . . . your lunch now, Mr Q."

"If there's no objection," he replied, "I'd prefer to go down to the cafeteria. Do you suppose they're serving consommé with poached plover eggs or a salpicon of mussels today?"

Mrs Toodle looked alarmed and hurried out. Qwilleran chuckled. He was feeling euphoric after his brief brush with amnesia.

Before going in search of food he combed his hair and thought about Mrs Cobb's remark: *The sheriff found the bicycle in the ditch!* The drainage ditch was a good thirty feet from the pavement to allow for future widening of the new highway. If he had blacked out or if he had hit some obstruction, he and his bike would have toppled over on the gravel shoulder. How did the bicycle end up in the ditch? It was a question he might pursue later, but first he needed food.

Wearing his Mackintosh bathrobe, Qwilleran headed for the elevator, walking with a slow and dignified step dictated by his legful of bandages. He was thankful he had not landed on his bad knee. On second thought, he realized he now might have two bad knees.

Everyone in the corridor seemed to know him.

Orderlies and ambulatory patients greeted him by name — or, rather, by initial — and one of the nurses said, "Sorry about your room, Mr Q — the color of the walls, I mean. It was supposed to be antique pink, but the painters got their signals crossed."

"It's not very appetizing," Qwilleran agreed. "It looks like raw veal, but I can live with it for another twenty-four hours."

In the cafeteria he was greeted with applause from the nurses, technicians, and doctors who were lunching on cottage cheese salads, bowls of chili, and braised cod with poached celery. He acknowledged their greetings with courtly bows and exaggerated salutes before taking his place in line. Ahead of him was a white-haired country doctor with two claims to fame: he was Melinda's father, and he had swabbed throats, set bones, and delivered babies for half of Moose County.

Dr Halifax Goodwinter turned and said, "Ah! The celebrated cyclist! Glad to see you're still among the living. It would be a pity if my daughter lost her first and only patient."

A nurse standing behind Qwilleran nudged his elbow. "You should wear a helmet, Mr Q. You could've been killed."

He carried a tray of chili and corn muffins to a table occupied by three men he had met at the Pickax Boosters Club: the hospital administrator, a genial urologist, and a banker who served on the hospital board of trustees.

The doctor said, "Planning to sue anybody, Qwill? I can steer you to a couple of ingenious ambulance chasers."

The banker said, "You can't sue the manufacturer. That kind of bike hasn't been made for fifty years."

The administrator said, "We're taking up a collection to buy you a new bike — and maybe a new bathrobe."

Patting the lapels of his ratty red plaid, Qwilleran said in his best declamatory style, "This is a vintage robe with a noteworthy provenance, gentlemen. The distress marks merely add to its associative value." The truth was that Koko had gone through a wool-eating phase, nibbling chair upholstery, neckties, the Mackintosh robe, and other handy items.

Qwilleran felt at ease with the hospital badinage. It was the same kind of jocular roasting he had enjoyed at the *Daily Fluxion*. Everyone in Pickax City seemed to like him, and why not? He was an affable companion, a sympathetic listener, and the richest man in the county. He had no delusions on that score. As a feature writer for the *Fluxion* he had been courted by lobbyists, politicians, businessmen, and media hounds. He accepted their attentions graciously, but he had no delusions.

After lunch the lab took blood samples, and Qwilleran had an EKG, followed by another nap and another dream.

Again it was vivid — painfully so. He was climbing out of a ditch near a lonely highway. His clothing was soaked; his pants were torn; his legs were bleeding. Blood was trickling into his right eye as he stumbled onto the highway and started to walk. Soon a red car stopped, and someone in a blue shirt jumped out. It was Junior Goodwinter, the young managing editor of the *Pickax*

Picayune. Junior gave him a ride back to town and talked incessantly on the journey, but Qwilleran could say nothing. He struggled to answer Junior's questions, but he could find no words.

The dream ended abruptly, and the dreamer found himself sitting up in bed, sweating and shivering. He mopped his face and then reached for the telephone and called the newspaper office.

"Qwill! You pulled through!" shouted Junior into the phone. "When I picked you up yesterday, you weren't exactly dead, but you weren't alive either. We had the type all set up to print an obit if you kicked off."

"Thanks. That was decent of you," Qwilleran said.

"Are you hitting on all eight? You sound okay."

"They sewed me together, and I look like the Spirit of '76. Where was I when you picked me up, Junior?"

"On Ittibittiwassee Road, beyond the Buckshot mineshaft. You were wandering around in the middle of the pavement in a daze — going in the wrong direction. Your clothes were all ripped and muddy. Your head was bleeding. You really had me worried, especially when you couldn't talk."

"Did you see my bike?"

"Tell the truth, I wasn't looking for it. I just concentrated on getting you to the hospital. I hit a hundred ten."

"What were you driving?"

"My Jag, luckily. That's why I could kick it up to one-ten so fast."

"Thanks, Junior. Let's have lunch next week. I'll buy."

Another dream checked out! Even the color of the car was accurate. Qwilleran knew that Junior's Jaguar was red.

He discussed his dreams with Melinda Goodwinter and Arch Riker that evening when they came to the hospital to have dinner with him in the cafeteria. Without her white coat and stethoscope Melinda looked more like the young woman he had been dating for the last two months.

Qwilleran asked her, "Do you kiss all your bedridden male patients?"

"Only those of advanced age," she retorted with a sweetly malicious look in her green eyes.

"Funny thing," he said, "but some of the details I couldn't remember came back to me in dreams this afternoon. There's only one blank left in my memory — the actual circumstances that caused the accident."

"It wasn't a pothole," Melinda said. "That's a brand-new highway, smooth as glass."

Riker said, "It's my guess that you swerved to avoid hitting something, Qwill, and skidded on the shoulder. A skunk or raccoon, perhaps, or even a deer. I saw a lot of dead animals on the road, coming in from the airport."

"We'll never know for sure," Qwilleran said. "How's everything at the house? Did you get some sleep? Did Mrs Cobb give you lunch? Did you see Koko?"

"Everything's fine. Koko met me at the front door and gave me a military inspection. I guess I passed muster, because he allowed me to enter."

Late that night, when the hospital corridor was silent,

Qwilleran dreamed his final dream. It was the missing link between the macaroni-and-cheese and the red Jaguar. He saw himself pedaling at a leisurely pace along a deserted highway, appreciating the smooth asphalt and the lack of traffic and the gently rolling hills. Pedaling uphill was easy, and coasting down was glorious.

He passed the abandoned Buckshot Mine with its rotting shaft house and ominous signs: *Danger* . . . *Keep Out* . . . *Beware of Cave-ins.* The deserted mines that dotted the lonely landscape around Pickax City were a source of endless fascination for Qwilleran. They were mysterious — silent — dead.

The Buckshot was different, however. He had been told that, if one listened intently, one could hear an eerie whistling sound coming from the shaft where eighteen miners had been buried alive in 1913.

In the dream he pedaled slowly and silently past the Buckshot. Only a tick-tick in the rear wheel and a grinding sound in the sprocket broke the stillness. He turned his head to gaze at the gray ghost of the shaft house . . . the sloping depression at the site of a cave-in . . . the vibrant green weeds that smothered the whole scene. He was staring so intently that he was unaware of a truck approaching from the opposite direction — unaware until its motor roared. He looked ahead in time to see its burst of speed, its sudden swerve into the eastbound lane, a murderous monster bearing down upon him. In the dream he had a vivid picture of the grille, a big rusty thing that seemed to be grinning. He yanked the handlebars and plunged down toward the roadside ditch, but the front wheel hit a rock and he went sailing over the handlebars. For an interminable moment he was airborne.

Qwilleran wrenched himself from sleep in a fright and found himself sitting up in bed, sweating and shouting.

An orderly hurried into the room. "Mr Q! Mr Q! What's the problem? A bad dream?"

Qwilleran shook himself in an effort to dispel the nightmare. "Sorry. Hope I didn't disturb the other patients."

"Want a drink of water, Mr Q?"

"Thanks. And will you raise the bed? I'd better sit up for a while."

Qwilleran leaned back against his pillow, reliving the dream. It was as graphic as the others. The sky was blue. The weeds around the deserted mine were poison green. The truck had a rusted grille.

Like the other dreams, it had actually happened, he realized, but there was no one he could phone for verification.

One thing was clear. What happened on Ittibittiwassee Road was no accident. He thought, I'm well liked in Pickax . . . but not by everyone.

CHAPTER TWO

It was midsummer when the richest man in Moose County fell off his antiquated bicycle. Two months before that incident he was far from affluent. He was an underpaid feature writer working for a large midwestern newspaper noted for its twenty-four-point bylines and meager wage scale. As a rugal bachelor he lived in a one-room furnished apartment and was making payments on a used car. He owned a fifty-year-old typewriter with a faulty shift key, and his library consisted of the odd titles found on the twenty-five-cent table in secondhand bookstores. His wardrobe, such as it was, fitted comfortably in two suitcases. He was perfectly content.

Jim Qwilleran's sole extravagance was the care and feeding of two Siamese cats who shunned catfood, preferring beef tenderloin, lobster, and oysters in season. Not only did they have aristocratic sensibilities and epicurean appetites, but Koko, the male, showed unusual intelligence. Tales of his extrasensory perception had made him legendary at the *Daily Fluxion* and the Press Club, although nothing of the cat's remarkable attribute was mentioned outside the profession.

Then, without ever buying a lottery ticket, Qwilleran

became a multimillionaire virtually overnight. It was a freak inheritance, and he was the sole heir.

When the astonishing news reached him, Qwilleran and his feline companions were vacationing in Moose County, the northern outpost of the state. They were staying in a lakeshore cabin near the resort town of Mooseville. As soon as he recovered from the shock he submitted his resignation to the *Daily Fluxion* and made arrangements to move to Pickax City, the county seat, thirty miles from Mooseville.

But first he had to clean out his desk at the *Fluxion* office, say goodbye to fellow staffers, and have one last lunch with Arch Riker at the Press Club.

The two men walked to the club, mopping their brows and complaining of the heat. It was the first hot spell of the season.

Qwilleran said, "I'm going to miss you and all the other guys, Arch, but I won't miss the hot weather. It's ninety-five degrees at City Hall."

"I suppose the photographers are frying their annual egg on the sidewalk," Arch remarked.

"In Moose County there's always a pleasant breeze. No need for air-conditioning."

"That may be, but how can you stand living four hundred miles from civilization?"

"Are you under the impression that today's cities are civilized?"

"Qwill, you've spent less than a month in that northern wilderness," Arch said, "and already you're thinking like a sheep farmer . . . Okay, I'll rephrase that question.

How can you stand living four hundred miles from the Press Club?"

"It's a gamble," Qwilleran admitted, "but those are the terms of Miss Klingenschoen's will: live in Moose County for five years or forfeit the inheritance."

At the club, where the air conditioner was out of commission, they ordered corned beef sandwiches, gin and tonic for Riker, and iced tea for Qwilleran.

"If you forfeit the inheritance," Riker went on, "who gets it?"

"Some outfit in New Jersey. I don't mind telling you, Arch, it was a tough decision for me to make. I wasn't sure I wanted to give up a job on a major newspaper for *any* amount of money."

"Qwill, you're unique — if not demented. No one in his right mind would turn down millions."

"Well, you know me, Arch. I like to work. I like newspapering and press clubs. I've never needed a lot of dough, and I've never wanted to be encumbered by possessions. It remains to be seen if I'll be comfortable with money — I mean Money with a capital *M*."

"Try!" Riker advised. "Try real hard. What are the encumbrances that might ruin your life?"

"Some complicated investments. Office buildings and hotels on the East Coast. A couple of shopping malls. Acreage in Moose County. Half of Main Street in Pickax City. Also the Klingenschoen mansion in Pickax and the log cabin in Mooseville where we spent our vacation."

"Rotten luck."

"Do you realize I'll need a housekeeping staff, gardeners, maintenance men, and probably a secretary?

Not to mention an accountant, a financial adviser, two attorneys, and a property management firm? That's not my style! They'll expect me to join the country club and wear tailor-made suits!"

"I'm not worried about you, Qwill. You'll always be your own man. Anyone who's convinced his cat is psychic will never conform to conventional folkways . . . Here's the mustard. Want horseradish?"

Qwilleran grunted and squirted a question mark of mustard on his corned beef.

Riker went on. "You'll never be anything but what you are, Qwill — a lovable slob. Do you realize every one of your ties is full of moth holes?"

"I happen to like my ties," Qwilleran countered. "They were all woven in Scotland, and they're not moth-eaten. Before Yum Yum came to live with us, Koko was frustrated and started chewing wool."

"Are those two cats playing house? I thought they were both neutered."

"Yes, but Siamese crave companionship. Otherwise they get neurotic. They do strange things."

"If you ask me," Riker said, "Koko is still doing some very strange things."

At that moment two photographers from the *Fluxion* stopped at the table to commiserate with Qwilleran. "Man, do you know what you're getting into up north?" one of them said. "Moose County is a *low-crime* area!"

"No problem," Qwilleran replied. "They import an occasional felon from down here, just so the cops won't get bored."

He was accustomed to being ribbed about his interest in crime. Everyone at the Press Club knew he had helped the police crack a few cases, and everyone knew that it was Koko who actually sniffed out the clues.

Qwilleran applied his attention to his sandwich again, and Riker resumed his questioning. "What's the population of Pickax?"

"Three thousand persons and four thousand pickup trucks. I call it Pickup City. The town has one traffic light, fourteen mediocre restaurants, a nineteenth-century newspaper, and more churches than bars."

"You could open a good restaurant and start your own paper, now that you're in the bucks."

"No thanks. I'm going to write a book."

"Any interesting people up there?"

"Contrary to what you think, Arch, they're not all sheep farmers. During my vacation I met some teachers and an engineer and a lively blond postmistress (married, unfortunately) and a couple of attorneys — brother and sister, very classy type. Also there's a young doctor I've started dating. She has the greenest eyes and longest eyelashes you ever saw, and she's giving me the come-on, if I'm reading the signals right."

"How come you always attract women half your age? Must be the overgrown moustache."

Qwilleran stroked his upper lip smugly. "Dr Melinda Goodwinter, MD . . . not bad for a Saturday night date."

"Sounds like a character in a TV series."

"Goodwinter is the big name in Moose County. There's half a page of them in the telephone directory, and the whole phone book is only fourteen pages thick. The Goodwinters go back to the days when fortunes were being made in mining."

"What supports the economy now?"

"Commercial fishing and tourism. A little farming. Some light industry."

Riker chewed his sandwich in somber silence for a while. He was losing his best writer as well as his lunchtime companion. "Suppose you move up there, Qwill, and then change your mind before the five years are up? What happens then?"

"Everything goes to the people in New Jersey. The estate is held in trust for five years, and during that time all I get is the income . . ."

"Which amounts to . . ."

"After taxes, upwards of a million, annually."

Riker choked on the dill pickle. "Anyone should . . . be able to . . . scrape by with that."

"You and Rosie ought to come up for a week. Fresh air — no hustle — safe environment. I mean, they don't have street crime and random killings in Pickax." He signaled the waitress for the check. "Don't expect me to pay for your lunch today, Arch. I haven't seen a penny of that inheritance yet. Sorry I can't stay for coffee. Gotta get to the airport."

"How long does it take to fly up there?"

"Forever! You have to change planes twice, and the last one is a hedgehopper."

After some quick handshaking and backslapping with denizens of the Press Club, Qwilleran accepted a sizable doggie bag from the kitchen and said a reluctant farewell to his old hangout. Then he caught the three o'clock plane.

In flight his thoughts went to Arch Riker. They had been friends long enough to have genuine concern for each other, and today Arch had been unduly morose. The editor usually exhibited the detached cool of a veteran deskman, punctuated with good-natured raillery, but today something was bothering him. Qwilleran sensed that it was more than his own departure for the north country.

The flight was uneventful, the landing was smooth; and in the pasture that served as the airport's long-term parking lot, his car was waiting as he had left it. No one had slashed the tires or jimmied the trunk. Driving from the airport he knew he was back in Moose County; pickup trucks — many of them modified for rough terrain — outnumbered passenger cars two to one.

The temperature was ideal. Qwilleran was glad to escape the city heat and city traffic. As he neared Mooseville, however, he began to feel the familiar anxiety: what might have happened in his absence?

He had left Koko and Yum Yum alone in the cabin on the lakeshore. A cat-sitter had promised to visit twice a day to feed them, give them fresh drinking water, and make polite conversation. But how reliable was the woman? Suppose she had broken a leg and failed to show up! Would the cats have enough water? How long could they live without food? Suppose she had carelessly let them out of the cabin and they had run away! They were indoor cats — city cats. How would they survive in the woods? What defense would they have against a predatory owl or hawk? Suppose there were wolves in the woods! Koko would fight to the death, but little Yum Yum was so timid, so helpless . . .

It was a highly nervous man who arrived at the cabin and unlocked the door. There they were — both cats sitting on the hearth rug, rump to rump, like bookends. They looked calm and contented and rather fat around the middle.

"You scoundrels!" he shouted. "You conned her into giving you too much food! You've been gorging!"

It was July, and the strong evening sun slanted into the cabin, backlighting the cats' fur and giving each of the reprobates an undeserved halo. With brown legs tucked confidently under fawn bodies, with brown ears cocked at an impudent angle, with blue eyes gazing inscrutably from brown masks, Koko and his accomplice defied Qwilleran to criticize their Royal Catnesses.

"You don't intimidate me in the slightest," he said, "so wipe that superior look off your face — both of you! I have news for you two characters. We're moving to Pickax in the morning."

The Siamese were staunch supporters of the status quo and always resented a change of address. Nevertheless, early the next morning Qwilleran packed them and their belongings into the car and drove them — protesting at the rate of forty howls per mile — to the Klingenschoen mansion, thirty miles inland.

The historic K mansion, as the locals called it, was situated on the Pickax Circle, that bulge in Main Street that wrapped around a small park. On the perimeter were two churches, the Moose County Courthouse, and the

Pickax Library, but none was more imposing than the hundred-year-old Klingenschoen residence.

Large, square, and solidly built of glistening fieldstone, it rose regally from well-kept lawns. A circular driveway served the front entrance, and a side drive led to the carriage house in the rear, also built of fieldstone with specks of quartz that sparkled in the sun.

Qwilleran drove to the back door of the house. He knew it would be unlocked, according to the friendly Pickax custom.

Hurriedly he carried two squirming animals into the big kitchen, placed their blue cushion on top of a refrigerator, and pointed out the adjoining laundry room as the new location of their drinking water and their commode. Cautioning them to be good, he closed both kitchen doors and then brought in the rest of his baggage, glancing frequently at his watch. He carried his two suitcases upstairs, and piled his writing materials on the desk in the library, including his ancient typewriter and a thirteen-pound unabridged dictionary with a tattered cover.

Previously Qwilleran had been impressed by the lavish furnishings of the mansion, but now he saw it with a proprietary eye: the high-ceilinged foyer with grandiose staircase; the dining room that could seat sixteen; the drawing room with its two fireplaces, two giant crystal chandeliers, and ponderous antique piano; the solarium with its three walls of glass. The place would cost a fortune to heat, he reflected.

Precisely at the appointed hour the doorbell rang, and he admitted the attorneys for the estate: Goodwinter &

Goodwinter, a prestigious third-generation law firm. The partners — Alexander and his sister Penelope — were probably in their mid-thirties, although their cool magisterial manner made them appear older. They shared the patrician features and blond hair characteristic of Goodwinters, and they were conspicuously well dressed for a town like Pickax, dedicated to jeans, T-shirts, and feed caps.

"I just arrived myself," said Qwilleran, breathing hard after his recent exertion. "We're now official residents of Pickax. I flew up from Down Below last night." In Pickax parlance, Down Below referred loosely to the urban sprawl in the southern half of the state.

"May we welcome you to Moose County," Alexander Goodwinter said pompously, "and I believe I speak for the entire community. By establishing yourself here without delay, you do us a great favor. Your presence will ameliorate public reaction to the Klingenschoen testament, a reaction that was not exactly — ah — favorable. We appreciate your thoughtful cooperation."

"My pleasure," Qwilleran said. "Shall we go into the library to talk?"

"One moment!" Alexander raised a restraining hand. "The purpose of our visit," he continued in measured tones, "is simply to make your transition as comfortable as possible. Unfortunately, I must emplane for Washington, but I leave you in the capable hands of my sister."

That arrangement suited Qwilleran very well. He found the junior partner a fascinating enigma. She was gracious, but haughtily so. She had a dazzling smile and provocative dimples, but they were used solely for business purposes. Yet, on one occasion he had found her quite relaxed, and the only clue to her sudden friendliness had been a hint of minty breath freshener. Penelope piqued his curiosity; she was a challenge.

In making his departure Alexander concluded, "Upon my return you must break bread with us at the club, and perhaps you will allow me to recommend my barber, tailor, and jeweler." He cast a momentary glance at his client's well-worn sweatshirt and untrimmed moustache.

"What I really need," Qwilleran said, "is a veterinarian — for preventive shots and dental prophylaxis."

"Ah . . . well . . . yes, of course," said the senior partner.

He drove away to the airport, and Qwilleran ushered Penelope into the library, enjoying the scent she was wearing — subtly feminine yet not unprofessional. He noted her silky summer suit, exquisitely tailored. She could pass for a fashion model, he thought. Why was she practicing law in this backwoods town? He looked forward to researching the question in depth.

In the library the warm colors of Bokhara rugs, leather seating, and thousands of books produced a wraparound coziness. The attorney took a seat on a blood-red leather sofa, and Qwilleran joined her there. Quickly she placed her briefcase on the seat between them.

"This will be an inspiring place in which to do your writing," she said, glancing at the bookshelves and the busts of Shakespeare and Homer. "Is that actually your typewriter? You might consider treating yourself to a word processor, Mr Qwilleran."

Being frugal by nature, he resented advice on how to spend his own money, but his irritation was lessened by Penelope's dimpled smile.

Then she frowned at the big book with tattered cover. "You could use a new dictionary, too. Yours seems to have had a great deal of use."

"That happens to be the cats' scratching pad," Qwilleran said. "There's nothing better than an unabridged dictionary, third edition, for sharpening the claws."

The attorney's aplomb wavered for an instant before she recovered her professional smile and opened her briefcase. "The chief reason for this meeting, Mr Qwilleran, is to discuss financial arrangements. Point One: Although the estate will not be settled for a year or more, we shall do everything in our power to expedite the probate. Meanwhile, our office will handle all expenses for household maintenance, employee wages, utilities, taxes, insurance, and the like. Invoices will come directly to us, obviating any inconvenience to you.

"Point Two: You have been good enough to sever ties with the *Daily Fluxion* and take up residence here immediately, and in so doing you have curtailed your income from that source. Accordingly we have arranged with the bank to provide a drawing account of several thousand a month until such time as the estate is settled — after which the monthly cash flow will be considerably greater. We can work out the terms of the drawing account with Mr Fitch, the trust officer at the bank. If you have need of a new car, he will arrange it. Is that agreeable, Mr Qwilleran?"

"It seems fair," he said casually.

"Point Three: Our office will arrange for landscape and maintenance services, but you will need a live-in housekeeper plus day help, and the choice of such personnel should be your own. Our secretary will be glad to send you applicants for these positions."

Qwilleran sat facing the door, and he was surprised to see a cat walk past the library with perpendicular tail and purposeful step. Both animals had been penned in the kitchen and yet Koko had easily opened a door and was exploring the premises.

"Point Four: The servants' quarters in the carriage house have been neglected and should be renovated — at the expense of the estate, of course. Would you be willing to work with our interior designer on the renovation?"

"Uh . . . yes . . . that would be fine," said Qwilleran. He was taking a mental inventory of breakables in the house and expecting to hear a shattering crash at any moment.

"Do you have any questions, Mr Qwilleran? Is there anything we can do for you?"

"Yes, Miss Goodwinter," he said, wrenching his attention away from the impending catastrophe. "I would like to make my position clear. Point One: I have no desire for a lot of money. I don't want a yacht or private jet. I'm not interested in reading the line print or watching the bottom line. All I wish is time to do some writing without too much interruption or annoyance."

The attorney appeared cautiously incredulous.

"Point Two, Miss Goodwinter: When the estate is

settled, I intend to establish a Klingenschoen Foundation to distribute the surplus income within Moose County. Organizations and individuals would be eligible to apply for grants, scholarships, business development loans — you know the kind of thing."

"Oh, Mr Qwilleran! How incredibly generous!" cried the attorney. "What a brilliant idea! I can hardly express what this will do for the morale and economic health of the county! And it will pacify the groups that had been promised bequests and then been disappointed. May we announce your proposal in the newspaper at once?"

"Go ahead. I'll count on your office to work out the details. We might start with an Olympic-size swimming pool for the high school, and I know the marine history buffs want backing for an underwater preserve, and the public library hasn't had a new book since *Gone with the Wind*."

"When Alex returns, your proposal will be the first item on our agenda. I'll telephone him in Washington tonight to break the good news."

"That brings me to Point Three," Qwilleran said genially. "May I take you to lunch?"

"Thank you, Mr Qwilleran. I would enjoy it immensely, but unfortunately I have a previous luncheon engagement." The dimpling process had subsided abruptly.

"How about dinner some evening this week?"

"I wish I could accept, but I'll be working late while Alex is out of town. Double work load, you know. Another time, perhaps."

As she spoke, a snatch of music came from the

drawing room — a few clear notes played on the antique piano.

"Who is that?" she inquired sharply.

"One of my feline companions," Qwilleran said with amusement. "That's just the white keys. Wait till he discovers the black ones."

The attorney glanced at him askance.

The sound had not surprised Qwilleran. He knew that Koko would never jump on the keyboard with a discordant crash. That approach was for ordinary cats. No, Koko would stand on his hind legs on the piano bench and stretch to reach the keys, pressing a few of them experimentally with a slender velvet paw. Having satisfied his curiosity, he would jump down and go on to his next investigation.

What Koko had played was a descending progression of four notes: G, E, C, G. Qwilleran knew the notes of the scale. As a boy he had practiced piano when he would have preferred batting practice. Now he recognized the tune as the opening phrase of "A Bicycle Made for Two."

"That piano rendition leads me to Point Four," he said to the attorney. "The doors in this house are so old that they don't latch securely. I'd like to be able to confine the Siamese to the kitchen on occasion."

"No problem at all, Mr Qwilleran," she said. "We'll send Birch Trevelyan to do the necessary repairs. You will find him an excellent workman, but you must be patient. He would rather go fishing than work."

"Another thing, Miss Goodwinter. I know Pickax considers it unfriendly to lock the back door, but this house is filled with valuables. Now that tourists are coming up here from Down Below, you never know who will prowl around and get ideas. You people in the country are entirely too trusting. The back door here has a lock but no key."

"A new lock should be installed," she said. "Discuss it with Birch Trevelyan. Feel free to ask him about any problem that arises."

Later Qwilleran wondered about her real reason for declining to dine. Most young women welcomed his invitations. He preened his moustache at the recollection of past successes. Was Penelope maintaining professional distance from a client? His doctor was eager for his invitations; why not his attorney? He also wondered why she flicked her tongue across her lips whenever she mentioned Birch what's-his-name.

After she left, he found Koko in the dining room, sniffing the rabbits and pheasants carved in deep relief on the doors of the huge sideboard. Yum Yum had crept cautiously from the kitchen and was exploring the solarium with its small forest of rubber plants, cushioned wicker chairs, and panoramic view of birdlife.

Qwilleran himself went to inspect the fieldstone building that had once stabled horses and housed carriages. Now there were stalls for four automobiles. Besides his own small car and the Klingenschoen limousine there was a rusty bicycle with two flat tires, and there was a collection of garden implements completely foreign to an apartment dweller from the Concrete Belt.

Climbing the stairs to the loft, he found two

apartments. In the days when servants were plentiful, these rooms would have been occupied by two couples — perhaps butler and cook, housekeeper and chauffeur. In the first apartment the drab walls and shabby furniture made a sorry contrast with the grandeur of the main house . . . But the second apartment!

The second apartment burst upon the senses like an explosion. The walls and ceiling were covered with graffiti in every color available in a spray can. Giant flowers that looked like daisies were sprayed on every surface, intertwined with hearts, initials, and references to "LUV."

There was so much personality expressed in this tawdry room that Qwilleran half expected to meet the former occupant coming out of the shower. What would she look like? "Dizzy blonde" was the phrase that came instantly to mind, but he dismissed it as archaic. No doubt she dyed her hair green and wore hard-edge makeup. On second thought, it was difficult to imagine green hair in Pickax, and certainly not on a housemaid at the K mansion.

How could anyone live in such a cocoon of wild pattern? Still, there was artistry in its execution. The motifs were organized as thoughtfully as a paisley shawl or Oriental rug.

Qwilleran knew that the previous owner had employed only a houseman, so . . . who was this unknown artist? How long ago had she painted these supergraphic daisies?

He touched his moustache; it always bristled when he made a discovery of significance. And now he was recalling the tune Koko had played on the piano. He hummed the four notes, and the lyric ran through his mind. *Daisy, Daisy!* An amazing coincidence, he thought. Or was it a coincidence?

CHAPTER THREE

The three new residents of the K mansion were systematically adjusting to their drastically altered environment. Qwilleran found a bedroom suite to his liking — eighteenth-century English with Chippendale highboys and lowboys and a canopied bed — and he was learning to heat water for instant coffee in the vast, well-equipped kitchen. Yum Yum claimed the solarium as her territory. Koko, the investigator, after inspecting the luxurious precincts upstairs and downstairs, finally selected the staircase as his special domain. From this vantage point he could watch the front door, keep a constant check on the foyer, monitor traffic, guard the approach to the second floor, and listen for promising sounds in the kitchen. He was sitting on the stairs in a comfortable bundle when applicants for the housekeeping position began to arrive.

Qwilleran, during his career in journalism, had interviewed prime ministers, delivery boys, Hollywood starlets, vagrants, elderly widows, rock stars, convicted rapists, and — he had forgotten what else. He had never interviewed, however, a prospective employee.

"You've got to help me screen them," he said to Koko. "She should be fond of cats, cook fairly well, know how to care for antiques, and be agreeable. But not *too* agreeable."

Koko squeezed his eyes shut in approval and assent.

The first applicant was a white-haired woman with an impressive resumé and excellent references, but she could no longer lift anything, walk up stairs, or stand on her feet for any length of time.

The second interviewee took one look at the staircase and screamed, "Is that a cat? I can't stand cats!"

"So far we're batting zero," Qwilleran said to his monitor on the stairs, and then the third applicant arrived.

She was a rosy-cheeked, clear-eyed young woman in jeans and T-shirt, obviously strong and healthy in every way. Her plodding gait indicated she was more accustomed to walking over a plowed field than an Oriental rug. Qwilleran could picture her milking a herd of cows, feeding a kitchenful of farmhands at harvesttime, and frolicking in the hayloft.

The interview took place in the reception area of the foyer, where French chairs were grouped around the ornate console table under a carved gilt mirror. The young woman sat quietly on the edge of a Louis XV rococo bergère, but her eyes were in constant motion, taking in every detail of the foyer and its furnishings.

She gave her name as Tiffany. "This is a pretty house," she said.

"Do you have a surname?" Qwilleran inquired. "A last name?" he added when she hesitated.

"Trotter."

"And what experience have you had as a housekeeper?"

"I've done everything." Her eyes roamed up the staircase, around the amber-colored tooled leather walls of the foyer, and up and down the eight-foot tall case clock.

Qwilleran surmised that she was either a spy for the assessor's office or the advance woman for a ring of thieves from Down Below, disguised as a farmer's daughter. If anything dire happened in the near future, Tiffany Trotter would be the first suspect. The name was undoubtedly an alias.

"How long have you been doing housekeeping?" He guessed her age at not more than twenty.

"All my life. I kept house for my dad before he got married again."

"Are you working now?"

"Part-time. I'm a cow-sitter, and I help my dad with the haying."

"A cow-sitter?" Qwilleran was reluctant to appear naive. "Do you have many clients?"

She shrugged. "Off and on. Some people keep a family cow, and when they go on vacation I go twice a day to milk her and feed her and clean out. I'm taking care of the Lanspeaks' Jersey now. They went to Hawaii." For the first time during the interview Tiffany showed enthusiasm, looking Qwilleran full in the face with her eyes sparkling. "I like Jerseys. This one has lots of personality. Her name is Stephanie."

The family she mentioned owned the local department

store. "Why would the Lanspeaks want to keep a cow?" Qwilleran asked.

"Fresh milk tastes better," she replied promptly and with conviction. "And they like homemade butter and homemade cheese."

Tiffany left her telephone number and drove away in a pickup truck.

Next came a Mrs Fulgrove, a scrawny woman who virtually vibrated with energy or nervousness. Without waiting for questions, she said, "I ain't aimin' to be a live-in housekeeper 'cause 'twouldn't be right, you bein' a single man and me a widow, but seein' as how they said you ain't a drinkin' man, I'd be willin' to clean and iron three days a week, which I worked here when the Old Lady was alive and I had to do the work of two seein' as how the reg'lar girl wouldn't lift a finger if I didn't snitch on her to the Old Lady, which the young ones today drink and smoke and dance and all that, and I'm glad I was born when folks had some self-respect, so I always work six days a week and go to church three times on Sunday."

Qwilleran said, "Your industry and dedication are to your credit, Mrs Fulgrove. What did you say was the name of the regular girl who was so lazy?"

"She was one of them Mull girls, which the Mulls was never respectable, not that I want to gossip, bein' a charitable woman if I do say it myself, and the Old Lady was fixin' to fire her, but she up and left of her own will, leavin' her rooms in an awful mess with the devil's own pictures painted all over the walls and dirt most everywhere, which the Old Lady was mad as a hornet, but 'twas good riddance, not that I'm sayin' she was wild, like others do, but she gallivanted around and stayed up late and wouldn't work, which I had to clean out her rooms after she run away."

After the woman had given a telephone number — a neighbor's, not her own — she left the house with a determined step, looking neither this way nor that. Immediately Qwilleran felt a strong desire to revisit the apartment with the devilish pictures. He knew there was an island of Mull off the coast of Scotland, and if the young woman happened to be Scottish, she couldn't be totally reprehensible.

In the garage loft he studied the initials scattered among the daisies and hearts on the walls and ceilings: BD, ML, DM, TY, RR, AL, WP, DT, SG, JK, PM, and more. If these were the men in her life, she had been a busy girl. On the other hand, they might be the fabric of fantasy. RR might be a movie star, or a president.

Back at his desk in the library he looked up Mull in the fourteen-page telephone directory, but the name was not listed. Forty-two Goodwinters but no Mulls. He telephoned Penelope.

"Miss Goodwinter, you're right about the servants' quarters. How do I get in touch with your interior designer?"

"Her name is Amanda Goodwinter, and our secretary will ask her to call you for an appointment," the attorney said. "Did you see the announcement of the Klingenschoen Foundation in yesterday's *Picayune*?"

"Yes, and it was very well stated. Have you had any reaction?"

"Everyone is delighted, Mr Qwilleran! They call it the best news since the K Saloon closed in the 1920s. When my brother returns, we shall explore the ramifications. Meanwhile, have you interviewed any prospective housekeepers?"

"I have, and will you tell your secretary not to send us any more octogenarians or ailurophobes or cow-sitters? By the way, do you know who painted the graffiti in the servants' quarters?"

"Oh, that atrocity!" Penelope exclaimed. "It was one of those girls from Dimsdale. She was housemaid for a short time."

"What happened to her? Did she get a job painting subway trains?"

"I hear she left town after defacing her apartment," the attorney said briskly. "Speaking of transportation, Mr Qwilleran, wouldn't you like to replace your little car with something more . . . upscale? Mr Fitch at the bank will cover the transaction."

"There's nothing wrong with the car I have, Miss Goodwinter. There's no rust on the body, and it's economical to operate."

Qwilleran ended the conversation hurriedly. While Penelope was talking he became aware of unusual noises coming from another part of the house — a miscellany of plopping, pattering, fluttering, swishing, and skittering. He rushed out of the library to track it down.

Beyond the foyer with its majestic staircase there was a vestibule of generous proportions, floored with squares of creamy white marble. Here was the rosewood hall stand with hooks for top hats and derbies, as well as a rack for walking sticks. Here was a marble-topped table with a silver tray for calling cards. And here was the massive front door with its brass handle and escutcheon, its brass doorbell that jangled when one turned a key on the outside, and its brass mail slot.

Through this slot were shooting envelopes of every size and shape, dropping in a pile on the floor. Sitting on the cool marble and watching the process with anticipation were Koko and Yum Yum. Now and then Koko would put forth a paw and scoop a letter from the pile, and Yum Yum would bat it around the slick floor.

As Qwilleran watched, the cascade of envelopes stopped falling, and through the sidelights he could see the mail carrier stepping into her Jeep and driving away.

His first impulse was to call the post office and suggest some other arrangement, but then he observed the pleasure that the event afforded the cats. They jumped into the pile like children in a snowbank, rolling over and skidding and scattering the mail. Nothing so wonderful had ever happened in their young lives! Letters slithered across the marble vestibule and into the parquet foyer, where Yum Yum tried to push them under the Oriental rug. Hiding things was her specialty.

One letter was gripped in Koko's jaws, and he paraded around with an air of importance. It was a pink envelope.

"Here, give me that letter!" Qwilleran commanded.

Koko ran into the dining room with Qwilleran in pursuit. The cat darted in and out of the maze of sixty-four chair legs, with the man chasing and scolding. Eventually Koko tired of the game and dropped the pink envelope at Qwilleran's feet.

It was a letter from the postmistress he had met in Mooseville during his vacation. Beautifully typed, it put to shame his own two-fingered efforts, which had not improved despite twenty-five years of filing news stories. The letter read:

Dear Qwill,

Congratulations on your good fortune! You and the Siamese will be a wonderful addition to Moose County. We hope you will enjoy living up here.

Nick and I have some exciting news, too. I'm pregnant at last! He wants me to quit my job because I'm on my feet so much (the doctor says I must be careful), so here's an idea. Could you use a part-time secretary? It would be fun to be a secretary to a real writer.

Say hello to Koko and Yum Yum for me.

Catfully yours,
Lori Bamba

It was obvious what had happened. Koko had selected the pink letter from the pile of mail because it carried the scent of someone he knew. Lori had established a rapport with the cats during their visit in Mooseville; they were entranced by her long golden braids tied with blue ribbons.

In a moment or two Koko appeared with another letter

and bounded away when Qwilleran reached for it. Then the chase was on — again.

"You think this is a game," Qwilleran shouted after him, "but it could get to be a bore! I'll start picking up my mail at the post office."

This time the letter was from a former landlady Down Below. One memorable winter Qwilleran had rented an apartment above her antique shop, in an old building that smelled of baked potatoes when the furnace was operating. Koko had recognized the scent of his former residence. The hand-written note read:

Dear Mr Qwilleran,

Rosie Riker told me about your inheritance, and I'm very happy for you, although we'll all miss your column in the *Daily Fluxion*.

Don't drop dead when I tell you I've sold my antique shop! My heart wasn't in the business after my husband died, so Mrs Riker is taking over. She's a smart collector, and she'd always wanted to be a dealer.

My son wants me to move to St Louis, but he's married now, and I might be in the way. Anyway, I got a crazy idea yesterday and stayed awake all night thinking about it. Here goes —

Mrs Riker says you inherited a big house full of antiques and will need a housekeeper. I can cook pretty well, you remember, and I know how to take care of fine antiques. Also — I have my appraiser's license now and could do some up-to-date appraisals for you — for insurance purposes. I'm serious! I'd love to do it. Let me know what you think.

Yours truly,
Iris Cobb

P.S. How are the cats?

Qwilleran's salivary glands went into action as he remembered Mrs Cobb's succulent pot roasts and nippy macaroni-and-cheese. He remembered other details: cheerful personality — dumpy figure — fabulous coconut cake. She believed in ghosts; she read palms in a flirtatious way; she left a few lumps in her mashed potatoes so they'd taste like the real thing.

He immediately put in a phone call to the urban jungle Down Below. "Mrs Cobb, your idea sounds great! But Pickax is a very small town. You might find it too quiet after the excitement of Zwinger Street."

Her voice was as cheerful as ever. "At my age I could use a little quiet, Mr Qwilleran."

"Just the same, you ought to look us over before deciding. I'll buy your plane ticket and meet you at the airport. How's the weather down there?"

"Sweltering!"

Koko had listened to the conversation with a forward tilt to his ears, denoting disapproval. Always protective of Qwilleran's bachelor status, he had resented the landlady's friendly overtures in the past.

"Don't worry, old boy," Qwilleran told him. "It's strictly business. And you'll get some home-cooked food for a change. Now let's open the rest of the mail."

The envelopes scattered about the vestibule included messages of welcome from five churches, three service clubs, and the mayor of Pickax. There were invitations to join the Ittibittiwassee Country Club, the Pickax Historical Society, the Moose County Gourmets, and a bowling league. The administrator of the Pickax Hospital asked Qwilleran to serve on the board of trustees. The superintendent of schools suggested that he teach an adult class in journalism.

Two other letters had been pushed under the rug in the foyer. The Volunteer Firefighters wished to make Qwilleran an honorary member, and the Pickax Singing Society needed a few more male voices.

"There's your chance," he said to the cat. Koko, as he grew older, was developing a more expressive voice with a gamut of clarion yowling, guttural growling, tenor yodeling, and musical yikking.

That afternoon Qwilleran met another Goodwinter. While writing about "beautiful living" for the *Daily Fluxion*, he had met all kinds of interior designers — the talented, the charming, the cosmopolitan, the fashionable, the witty, and the scheming, but Amanda Goodwinter was a new experience.

When he answered the doorbell — after three impatient rings — he found a scowling gray-haired woman in a baggy summer dress and thick-soled shoes, peering over her glasses to examine the paint job on the front door.

"Who painted this door?" she demanded. "They botched it! Should've stripped it down to the wood. I'm Amanda Goodwinter." She clomped into the vestibule without looking at Qwilleran. "So this is the so-called showplace of Pickax! Nobody ever invited me here."

He ventured to introduce himself.

"I know who you are! You don't need to tell me. Penelope says you need help. The foyer's not too bad, but it needs work. What fool put that tapestry on those chairs?" She prowled from room to room, making comments. "Is this the drawing room I've heard about? The draperies have got to go; they're all wrong . . . The dining room's too dark. Looks like the inside of a tomb."

Qwilleran interrupted politely. "The attorney suggested that you might redecorate the rooms over the garage."

"What!" she screeched. "You expect me to do servants' quarters?"

"As a matter of fact," he said, "I want to use one of the garage apartments myself — as a writing studio — and I'd like it done in good contemporary."

The designer was pacing back and forth in the foyer like a caged lioness. "There's no such thing as *good* contemporary! I don't do contemporary. I loathe the damn stuff."

Qwilleran cleared his throat diplomatically. "Are there any other designers in town who are competent to work with contemporary?"

"I'm perfectly competent, mister, to work in any style," she snapped.

"I don't want to upset you . . ."

"I'm *not* upset!"

"If you feel uncomfortable with contemporary, I know

designers Down Below who will undertake the entire commission, including the mansion itself after the garage apartments are finished."

"Show me the garage," she said with a scowl. "Where is it? How do we get out there?"

He showed her to the rear of the house. As she passed the library she gave a grunt of begrudging approval. She sniffed at the yellow and green breakfast room and called it gaudy. Poking her head into the kitchen, she stared without comment at the top of the refrigerator, where the Siamese were striking sculptural poses on their blue cushion.

In the garage they climbed the stairs to the loft, and Qwilleran pointed out the drab apartment he wanted converted to a studio.

"Hasn't been touched for twenty years," she grumbled. "Plaster's all shot. Needs a lot of work."

"If you think this one needs a lot of work," he said, "wait until you see the other suite."

Amanda gave one look at the daisy extravaganza and groaned. "Don't tell me! Let me guess! It was the Mull girl who did this. What a mess! She came to work here after I let her go."

"Did she work for you?"

"I paid her wages, dammit, but she didn't work! Her art teacher wanted me to take her on. Big mistake. Cute girl, but not a brain in her head. Her scruffy friends were always hanging around the studio, too. Then she got sticky fingers, so I gave her the sack. Those Mulls! Not a one of them ever amounted to anything . . . Look at this abomination! It'll take three coats to cover it, maybe four."

Koko's tune rang through Qwilleran's mind. *Daisy, Daisy*. "Hold everything," he said. "Forget this apartment for the time being and concentrate on my studio."

"You'll have to come downtown to pick out colors and look at samples," she said irritably.

"Let's make it easy. Just rip out the rugs and furniture and cart the whole shebang to the dump. Then carpet the floor in dark brown, like my shoes."

"Hmmm, you're a casual cuss," the designer said.

"And paint the walls the color of my pants."

"Mojave beige?"

"Whatever you call it. And let's have some of those adjustable blinds with thin slats. After that we'll talk about furniture."

After the designer had stomped down the stairs, mumbling to herself, Qwilleran had another look at the intricate daisy design and regretted the artist had left town. During his career as a crime reporter he had won the confidence of many characters outside the law — or on the borderline — and this girl, with her talent and her questionable reputation, interested him.

Daisy, Daisy. Fingering his moustache in perplexity, he wondered why and how Koko had touched those particular keys on the piano. True, the cat was fascinated by push buttons, switches, and typewriter keys, but this was the first piano Koko had ever seen, and he had played a recognizable tune.

Returning to the house, Qwilleran found something else to ponder. Koko, guarding the house from his post on the grand staircase, was sitting on the third stair. Out of a flight of twenty-one stairs, he always chose the third.

CHAPTER FOUR

No jets landed at the Pickax airport. There was no VIP lounge in the terminal — not even a cigarette machine for nervous passengers. Moose County travelers were grateful to have shelter and a few chairs.

While waiting for Mrs Cobb's plane, Qwilleran recalled that much of his education about antiques had come from the Cobbs' establishment when he was covering the "junk beat" for the *Daily Fluxion*. What he remembered of the lady herself was a composite of bustling exuberance, plump knees, and two pairs of eyeglasses dangling from ribbons around her neck.

When she stepped off the plane in her travel-weary pink pantsuit, he found her thinner and somewhat subdued, and her glasses had new frames studded with rhinestones.

"Oh, Mr Qwilleran, how good to see you!" she cried. "What lovely weather you have here! It's suffocating in the city. Isn't this a quaint airport!"

"Everything's quaint in Pickax, Mrs Cobb. Do you have luggage?"

"Only this carryon. It's all I need for an overnight."

"You're welcome to stay longer, you know."

"Oh, thank you, Mr Qwilleran, but I have to go back

tomorrow to close the deal with Mrs Riker. She's going to live in your old apartment over the shop."

"*She* is going to live there?" Qwilleran repeated. "What about her husband? What about their house in the suburbs?"

"Didn't you know? She's getting a divorce."

"I had lunch with Arch a few days ago, and he didn't say a word about it . . . but I remember he looked troubled. I wonder what happened."

"I'll let him tell you the story," Mrs Cobb said, and she pursed her lips with finality.

On a relentlessly straight highway they drove across the lonely landscape of Moose County — through evergreen forests and rockbound wasteland, past abandoned mines and unnatural hillocks that had once been slag heaps.

"Very rocky," Mrs Cobb observed.

"Pickax is built almost entirely of stone," said Qwilleran.

"Is it really? Tell me about your house. Is it sumptuous?"

"It's a big chunk of fieldstone three stories high. I call it Alcatraz Provincial," he began. "All the rooms are huge. The foyer would make a good roller rink if we took up the Oriental rugs . . . Every bedroom has a canopied bed and its own sitting room, dressing room, and bath . . . There's an English pub in the basement, and the top floor was supposed to be a ballroom, but it was never finished . . . The kitchen is so big you have to walk a mile to prepare a meal. It includes a butler's pantry, a food storage room, a laundry, a half bath, and a walk-in broom closet. The whole service area, as well as the solarium, is floored in square tiles of red quarry stone."

"Any ghosts?" Mrs Cobb asked with some of the old twinkle in her eyes. "Every old house should have a ghost. Maybe you remember the one we had on Zwinger Street. She never materialized, but she moved things around in the middle of the night. She was very prankish."

"I remember her very well," Qwilleran said. "She put salt shakers in your bedroom slippers." He also remembered that her ghostly pranks were an ongoing practical joke that C. C. Cobb had played on his gullible wife.

"How's Koko?" she asked.

"He's fine. He's taking piano lessons."

"Oh, Mr Qwilleran," she laughed. "I never know whether to believe what you say."

They approached Pickax via Goodwinter Boulevard, lined with the stately stone houses that wealthy mining pioneers had built in the heyday of the city. Then came Main Street, the circular park, and the majestic K mansion.

Mrs Cobb gave a little scream. "Is this it? Oh! Oh! I want the job!"

"You don't know how much it pays," Qwilleran said. "Neither do I."

"I don't care. I want the job."

When they entered the foyer, the amber walls were glowing and the brass-and-crystal chandelier was sparkling. The furnishings looked almost self-consciously pedigreed.

"Why, it's like a museum!"

"It's a little rich for my taste," Qwilleran admitted, "but everything is the real thing, and I have respect for it."

"I could do a real museum catalogue for you. That rosewood-and-ormolu console is Louis XV, and I'll bet it's a signed piece. The clock is a Burnap — brass works, moonphase, late eighteenth."

"Are you ready for the dining room?" Qwilleran switched on the twenty-four electric candles mounted on two staghorn chandeliers. It was a dark room, richly paneled, and the furniture was massive.

"Linenfold paneling!" Mrs Cobb gasped. "Austrian chandeliers! The furniture is German, of course."

"That's the original furniture," Qwilleran said, "before the Klingenschoens became serious collectors and switched to French and English."

When they crossed the foyer to the drawing room, she stared in awed silence. Chandeliers festooned with crystal were ablaze in the afternoon sun. Mellowed with age, the red walls made a handsome background for oil paintings in extravagant frames: French landscapes, Italian saints, English noblemen, and one full-length, life-size portrait of an 1880 beauty with bustle and parasol. On the far wall a collection of Chinese porcelains filled the shelves in two lofty arched niches.

"I think I'm going to faint," Mrs Cobb said.

"You should rest for a while," Qwilleran suggested. "There are four suites upstairs, each done in a different period. I'll bring your overnight bag up to the French suite in a few minutes."

While she climbed the stairs in a daze, he dashed off a note to his friend Down Below.

Dear Arch,

Mrs Cobb just broke the bad news. I don't need to tell you how terrible I feel about it. Why don't you take a week off and fly up here? It'll be a change of scene, and we can talk.

Qwill

He was addressing the envelope when he heard cries of alarm upstairs. "What are they doing? *What are they doing?*"

Mrs Cobb came rushing down the stairs, babbling incoherently, and he ran to meet her.

"That truck in the back drive!" she cried. "I looked out the window. They're stealing things from the garage. Stop them! Stop them!"

"Don't get excited, Mrs Cobb," Qwilleran said. "This isn't Zwinger Street. Those are porters from the design studio, cleaning out the junk before we redecorate."

"It's not junk! Stop them!"

They both hurried to the garage, where a truck was being loaded with rolled rugs, an old mattress, and odds and ends of furniture.

"That's a Hunzinger!" Mrs Cobb shouted, pointing to an odd-looking folding chair. "And that's a real Shaker rocker!" She rushed about — from an early trestle table to a Connecticut dower chest to a Pennsylvania German *Schrank*.

Qwilleran stopped the porters. "Take it all back except

the mattress. Put everything in one of the garage stalls until we can sort it out."

Mrs Cobb was weak with shock and excitement. "What a narrow escape," she said, over a cup of tea. "You know, there was a period when Americana wasn't appreciated. These people must have moved their heirlooms to the garage when they bought their French and English antiques. It's strange that your decorator didn't recognize their current value."

Maybe she did, Qwilleran thought.

Later in the afternoon he conducted the prospective housekeeper on a walking tour of downtown Pickax. "How do you like the French suite?" he asked.

"I've never seen anything so grand! There's a Norman bonnet-top armoire that must be early eighteenth century!" Hesitantly she added, "If I come to work here, would you mind if I did a few appraisals for other people on the side?"

"Not at all. You can even open a tearoom in the basement and tell fortunes."

"Oh, Mr Qwilleran, you're such a joker."

Downtown Pickax was a panorama of imitation Scottish castles, Spanish fortresses, and Cotswold cottages. "All real stone," he pointed out, "but somehow it looks fake, like a bad movie set."

They passed Amanda's studio (pure Dickens) and the offices of the *Pickax Picayune* (early monastery). Then he steered her into the office (Heidelberg influence) of Goodwinter & Goodwinter.

The junior partner was conferring with a client but consented to step out of her private office for a moment.

Qwilleran said, "I want to introduce Iris Cobb. I've convinced her to move up here from Down Below and manage our household. Mrs Cobb, this is Penelope Goodwinter, attorney for the estate."

"Pleased to meet you," said the housekeeper, extending her hand. Penelope, glancing at the rhinestone-studded glasses, was a fraction of a second slow in shaking hands and saying, "How nice."

Qwilleran went on. "Mrs Cobb is not only experienced in household management, but she's a licensed appraiser and will catalogue the collection for us."

His former landlady beamed, and Penelope said, "Oh, really? We must discuss salary, of course. When do you wish to start your employment, Mrs Cobb?"

"Well, I'm flying home tomorrow, and I'll drive up here in my van as soon as I pack my reference books."

"I suggest," the attorney said, "that you defer your arrival until your apartment is redecorated. At present it's in deplorable condition."

"No problem," Qwilleran interjected. "Mrs Cobb will have the French suite in the house. I plan to fix up the garage apartment for myself."

The attorney's reaction started with shock, faded into disapproval, and recovered enough to muster a half smile. "I hope you will both be comfortable. Let us talk about terms and contracts tomorrow."

"I'm taking Mrs Cobb to dinner at the Old Stone Mill tonight," Qwilleran said. "Would you care to join us?"

"Thank you. Thank you so much, but I have a previous engagement. And now . . . if you will excuse me . . ."

"Oh my!" Mrs Cobb said afterward. "She's a very smart dresser, isn't she? I didn't know they had clothes like that in Pickax."

Qwilleran reported the incident to Melinda Goodwinter after putting the housekeeper on the plane the next day. The young doctor with green eyes and long eyelashes telephoned to invite him to dinner.

"My treat," she said. "I'd like to take you to Otto's Tasty Eats."

"Never heard of it. How's the food?"

"Ghastly, but there's lots of it. It's a family restaurant — no liquor — and you can sit in the smoking section or the screaming section, depending on whether you want to ruin your lungs or your eardrums."

"You make the invitation irresistible, Melinda."

"To tell the truth, I have an ulterior motive. I want to see your house. I've never seen the interior. The Klingenschoens and the Goodwinters weren't on the same wavelength socially. Could you meet me at Otto's at six-fifteen? I'll reserve a booth."

At the appointed hour Qwilleran was wedging his green economy-model car into the crowded parking lot when Melinda pulled up in a silver convertible.

"When are you going to buy a gold-plated Rolls?" she greeted him.

"Do I look like a sheikh? Don't let the moustache mislead you."

"You really made a hit when you proposed giving away your money," she said. "There's a rumor that Pickax will be renamed Qwillville. All the women in Moose County will be chasing you, but remember — I found you first."

Otto's Tasty Eats occupied a former warehouse in the industrial area of Pickax. The wrinkled carpet suggested old army blankets. Long institutional tables — at least an acre of them — were covered with sheets of stiff white paper. Lights glared. Noise reverberated. Customers flocked in by the hundreds.

In the center of the room was a veritable shrine to gluttony: twelve-gallon crocks of watery soup, bushels of torn iceberg lettuce, mountains of fried chicken and fried fish, tubs of reconstituted mashed potatoes, and a dessert table that was a sea of white froth masquerading as whipped cream.

"Do you come here often?" Qwilleran asked.

"Only when I entertain supercilious urban types."

Overstuffed diners were making three or four trips to the buffet, but Melinda insisted on ordering from the menu and having table service.

"I don't imagine," Qwilleran said, "that your cousins from the law office are frequent diners at Otto's Tasty Eats." He described the meeting between the attorney and Mrs Cobb. "Penelope was a trifle perturbed when I told her the housekeeper would occupy the French suite and I'd live over the garage."

Melinda's green eyes brimmed with merriment. "She probably went into shock. She and Alex are the last of the hard-line Goodwinter snobs. They consider themselves the superior branch of the family. Did you know that Penny is the one with brains? Alex is just a tiresome bore with an inflated ego, and yet she defers to him as if he were the mastermind."

"He's a good-looking guy. Is he involved in politics? He seems to go to Washington a lot."

"Well, it's like this," Melinda explained. "There's a lot of Old Money in Moose County, and Alex steers campaign donations to friendly pols. He loves the importance it gives him in the Capitol and at Washington parties. Have you met any other Goodwinters?"

"Junior at the newspaper, for one. He's a bright kid, and he majored in journalism, but he's wasted at the *Picayune*. It looks like an antebellum weekly. I told him he's got to get the classified ads off the front page."

"I hear that cousin Amanda is going to redecorate your garage apartment. Did she kick you in the shins or just call you a twelve-letter word?"

"I don't understand how that woman stays in business. She has the personality of a hedgehog."

"She has a captive clientele. There's no other decorator within four hundred miles."

They could talk freely. Their booth was an island of privacy in a maelstrom of ear-splitting noise. The animated conversation of happy diners and the excited shrieks of children bounced off the steel girders and concrete walls, and the din was augmented by the Tasty Eats custom of pounding the table with knife handles to express satisfaction with the food.

The waiter was deferential. Melinda was not only a Goodwinter; she was a doctor. He brought a lighted candle to the table — a red stub in a smoky glass left over from Christmas. He persuaded the kitchen to *broil* two orders of pickerel *without breading*, and he found a few robust leaves of spinach to add to the sickly salad greens.

Qwilleran said to Melinda, "I wish you would do me a favor and explain the Goodwinter mystique."

"It's simple," she said. "We've been here for five generations. My great-great-grandfather was an engineer and surveyor. His four sons made fortunes in the mines. Most speculators grabbed their money and went to live abroad, so their daughters could marry titles, but the Goodwinters stayed here, always in business or the professions."

"Too bad none of them ever opened a good restaurant. Are there any black sheep in the family?"

"Occasionally, but they're always persuaded to move to Mexico or change their name."

"Change it to Mull, I suppose."

Melinda gave him an inquiring glance. "You've heard about the Mulls? That's an unfortunate social problem. They worked in the mines a hundred years ago, and their descendants have lived on public assistance for the last three generations. They lack motivation — drop out of school — can't find jobs."

"Where did they emigrate from originally?"

"I don't know, but they were miners when the pay was a dollar and a half a day. They worked with *candles* in their caps and had to buy their own candles from the company store. The miners were exploited by the companies and by the saloons. You can read about it in the public library."

"Did any of the Mulls ever break out of the rut?"

"The young ones often leave town, and no one ever

hears about them again — or cares. There's a lot of poverty and unemployment here. Also a lot of inherited wealth. Have you noticed the cashmeres at Scottie's Men's Store and the rocks at Diamond Jim's Jewelry? Moose County also has more private planes per capita than any other county in the state."

"What are they used for?"

"Mostly convenience. Commercial airlines have to route passengers in roundabout ways through hub cities. My dad flew his own plane before he became diabetic. Alex Goodwinter has a plane. The Lanspeaks have two — his and hers."

Melinda bribed the waiter to find some fresh fruit for dessert, and after coffee Qwilleran said, "Let's go to my place. I'd like to show you my graffiti."

Melinda brightened, and she batted her long lashes. "The evening begins to show promise."

They drove both cars to the K mansion, and she asked if she might park the silver convertible in the garage. "It would be recognized in the driveway," she explained, "and people would talk."

"Melinda, haven't you heard? This is the last quarter of the twentieth century."

"Yes, but this is Pickax," she said with raised eyebrows. "Sorry."

When Qwilleran escorted his guest upstairs to the servants' quarters, she walked into the jungle of daisies in a state of bedazzlement. "Ye gods! This is stupendous! Who did it?"

"A former housemaid. One of the Mulls. Worked for Amanda before she came here."

"Oh, *that one*! I guess she was a one-woman disaster at the studio. Amanda fired her for pilfering."

"After doing these murals she left town," Qwilleran said. "I hope she found a way to use her talent."

"It's really fantastic! It's hard to believe it was done by Daisy Mull."

"Daisy?" Qwilleran echoed in astonishment. "Did you say *Daisy* Mull?"

A melody ran through his mind, and he wondered if he should mention it. Previously he had hinted to Melinda about Koko's extrasensory perception, but a piano-playing cat seemed too radical a concept to share even with a broadminded MD.

"You've never met Koko and Yum Yum," he said. "Let's go over to the house."

When he conducted his guest into the amber-toned foyer, she gazed in wonder. "I had no idea the Klingenschoens owned such fabulous things!"

"Penelope knew. Didn't she ever tell you?"

"Penelope would consider it gossip."

"The rosewood-and-ormolu console is Louis XV," Qwilleran mentioned with authority. "The clock is a Burnap. Koko is usually sitting on the staircase to screen arriving visitors, but this is his night off."

Melinda commented on everything. The sculptured plaster ceilings looked like icing on a wedding cake. The life-size marble figures of Adam and Eve in the solarium had a posture defect caused by a calcium deficiency, she said. The Staffordshire dogs in the breakfast room were good examples of concomitant convergent strabismus.

"Want to see the service area?" Qwilleran asked. "The cats often hang out in the kitchen."

Yum Yum was lounging on her blue cushion on top of the refrigerator, and Melinda stroked her fur adoringly. "Softer than ermine," she said.

Koko was conspicuously absent, however.

"He could be upstairs, sleeping in the middle of a ten-thousand-dollar four-poster-bed," Qwilleran said. "He has fine taste. Let's go up and see."

While he hunted for the cat, Melinda inspected the suites furnished in French, Biedermeier, Empire, and Chippendale. Koko was not to be found.

Qwilleran was beginning to show his nervousness. "I don't know where he can be. Let's check the library. He likes to sleep on the bookshelves."

He ran downstairs, followed by Melinda, but there was no sign of the cat in any of his favorite places — not behind the biographies, not between the volumes of Shakespeare, not on top of the atlas.

"Then he's got to be in the basement."

The English pub had been imported from London, paneling and all, and it was a gloomy subterranean hideaway. They turned on all the lights and searched the bar, the backbar, and the shadows.

No Koko!

CHAPTER FIVE

Frantically Qwilleran scoured the premises for the missing Koko, with Melinda tagging along and offering encouragement.

"He'll be in one of four places," he told her. "A soft surface, or a warm spot, or a high perch, or inside something."

None of these locations produced anything resembling a cat. Calling his name repeatedly, they peered under sofas and beds, behind armoires and bookcases, and into drawers, cupboards, and closets.

Qwilleran dashed about with increasing alarm, looking in the refrigerator, the oven, the washer, the dryer, then the oven again.

"Slow down, Qwill. You're stressing." Melinda put a hand on his arm. "We'll find him. He's around here somewhere. You know how cats are."

"He's got to be in the house . . . unless . . . you know, the back door can't be locked. Someone could come in and snatch him. Or he might have eaten something poisonous and crawled away in a corner."

Melinda, wandering in aimless search, stepped into the back entry and called, "What's this stairway? Where does it go?"

"What stairway? I never noticed any stairway back there."

Hidden by the broom closet and closed off by a door that latched poorly, it was the servants' stairs to the second floor — a narrow flight with rubberized treads. Qwilleran bounded to the top, followed by Melinda, and they emerged in a hallway with a series of doors. Two doors stood ajar. One opened into a walk-in linen closet. The second gave access to another flight of ascending stairs, wide but unfinished and dusty. "The attic!" Qwilleran exclaimed. "It was supposed to be a ballroom. Never finished." Flipping wall switches, he scrambled to the top, sneezing. Melinda ventured up the stairs cautiously, shielding her mouth and nose with her hand.

The staircase ended in a large storage room illuminated faintly by fading daylight through evenly spaced windows and by eight low-wattage light bulbs dangling from the ceiling.

Qwilleran called the cat's name, but there was no answer. "If he's up here, how will we find him among all this junk?"

The space was littered with boxes, trunks, cast-off furniture, framed pictures, rolls of carpet, and stacks of old *National Geographics*.

"He could be asleep, or sick, or worse," he said.

"Could we lure him out with a treat?" Melinda suggested.

"There's a can of lobster in the food pantry. Open it and bring it up."

When she had run downstairs, Qwilleran stood still

and listened. The floorboards had stopped creaking. The hum of traffic on Main Street seemed far away. He held his breath. He could hear a familiar sound. What was it? He strained to listen. It was scratching — the whisper of claws gliding over a smooth surface. He followed the sound noiselessly.

There, in a far corner of the attic, stood a large carton, and Koko was on top of it with his hind end elevated and his front assembly stretched forward as he scratched industriously.

"Koko! What are you doing up here?" Qwilleran demanded in the consternation that followed his unnecessary panic. Then a prickling sensation on his upper lip caused him to investigate the scene of the action. A corrugated carton that had once contained a shipment of paper towels was tied with twine and labeled with a tag on which was a name in excellent handwriting: Daisy Mull.

By the time Melinda returned with the lobster, Qwilleran had untied the carton and was tossing out articles of clothing. "This is astonishing!" he shouted over his shoulder. "There's something important about this box, or Koko wouldn't have found it."

Out of the carton came a musty-smelling jacket of fake fur in black and white stripes unknown to any animal species, along with a woolly stocking hat that had once been white and a pair of high red boots with ratty fur trim. There were faded flannel shirts, well-worn jeans, two maid's uniforms, and a sweatshirt printed with the message: TRY ME. A small item wrapped in a wad of newspaper proved to be an ivory elephant with Amanda's studio label on the bottom of the teakwood base.

Qwilleran said, "Obviously she went south when she cleared out — to some climate where she wouldn't need winter clothing. Probably California. Dreamers always head for California, don't they? And she left her uniforms behind, so she didn't plan a career as a domestic."

"But why would she leave the elephant? If she liked it enough to steal it, wouldn't she like it enough to take it along? You can tell it's valuable."

"Smart question," Qwilleran said as he piled the clothing back into the carton. "You take the elephant; I'll carry Koko — if I can find him. Where did he go?"

Having finished the can of lobster, the cat was cleaning his mask, whiskers, ears, paws, chest, underside, and tail.

"Either he was trying to tell us something about Daisy Mull," Qwilleran said, "or he thought of a sneaky way to get an extra meal."

The three of them returned to the main floor, carefully closing the door to the attic stairs. It immediately popped open.

"That's typical of old buildings," Qwilleran complained. "The doors never fit properly. There are too many places for an inquisitive animal to get lost."

"He wasn't lost," Melinda said with a smug smile. "It's simply that you couldn't find him."

"For that astute observation you'll be rewarded with a nightcap. Would you like Scotch, bourbon, white grape juice, a split of champagne? I also have beer, in case Penelope's maintenance man ever shows up to fix the doors."

"What are you drinking?"

"Club soda with a twist."

"I'll have a split."

Qwilleran carried the tray of drinks into the library and slipped the ivory elephant into a desk drawer. "Would you enjoy some music? There's a prehistoric stereo here, and an odd assortment of records that you could use for paving a patio. This house came equipped with seven television sets, and I'd like to trade in six of them for a new music system."

"Don't you like TV?"

"I'm a print man. The printed word does more for me than the small screen."

After some grinding and humming and a loud *clunk* the record changer produced some romantic zither music, and they sat on the blood-red leather sofa that Qwilleran had recently shared with Penelope Goodwinter, but there was no briefcase between them and considerably less space.

He said, "Koko has an uncanny talent for finding objects of significance. I don't usually mention it because the average person wouldn't believe it, but I feel I can confide in you."

"Any time," Melinda said with an agreeable inflection in her voice.

"It's good to have a confidante." His mournful eyes met her inviting green gaze and the world stood still, but the magic moment was interrupted by a simulated catfight in the foyer. Qwilleran huffed into his moustache, and Melinda sipped her champagne and looked at the three walls of bookshelves.

"Nice library," she said.

"Yes. Good bindings."

"Mostly classics, I suppose."

"It appears so."

"Did the Klingenschoens read these?"

"I doubt it . . . . Melinda, did you ever see Daisy Mull? What did she look like?"

"Hmmm . . . tiny . . . reddish hair . . . pouty mouth. Daisy was quite visible in Pickax. She and her girlfriend used to stand outside the music store and giggle when cars tooted their horns. Her clothes were flashy by Pickax standards, but that was a few years ago. Things have changed. Today even the middle-aged women in Pickax have given up lavender sweater sets and basket bags."

Qwilleran draped an arm over the back of the sofa, musing that a firm, shiny, slippery upholstery left something to be desired. A loungy, down-filled, velvety sofa would be more seductive; at least, that had been his experience in the past.

"Why did you name your cats Koko and Yum Yum?" Melinda asked. "Are you a Savoyard?"

"Not especially, although I like Gilbert and Sullivan, and in college I sang in *The Mikado*."

"You're an interesting man, Qwill. You've lived everywhere and done everything."

He groomed his moustache self-consciously. "It helps if you've been around as long as I have. You've always dated young squirts from medical school."

"Not true! I'm always attracted to older men. Eyelids with a middle-aged droop turn me on."

He leaned closer to add champagne to her glass. There

was a sense of pleasurable propinquity, and then the tall case clock started to bong eleven times and Koko walked into the library. Walking with a stiff-legged gait and tail at attention, he looked at the pair on the sofa and uttered an imperious "YOW!"

"Hello, Koko," Melinda replied. "Are you and I going to be friends?"

Without a reply he turned and left the scene, and a moment later they heard another insistent howl.

"Something's wrong," Qwilleran said. "Excuse me." He followed the cat and found him in the vestibule, staring at the front door.

"Sorry, Koko. Wrong time of day. The mail comes in the afternoon."

Returning to the library, Qwilleran explained the cats' obsession with the mail slot. Casually he was maneuvering to resume the intimate mood that had been interrupted, when Koko stalked into the room a second time. Looking sternly at Melinda, he said, "nyik nyik nyik YOW!" And again he marched to the front door.

"Does he want to go out?"

"No, he's an indoor cat."

"He has a noble face, hasn't he?" She glanced at her watch.

"Siamese are a noble breed."

The third time Koko made his entrance, scolding and glaring at the guest, she said, "He's trying to tell me something." She jumped up and trailed after the determined animal, who plodded resolutely toward the front of the house, stopping at intervals and looking back to be sure she was following.

In the vestibule he stared pointedly at the door handle.

"Qwill, I believe he's telling me to go home."

"This is embarrassing, Melinda."

"That's okay. I have the early shift at the clinic tomorrow."

"My apology! He likes the lights turned out at eleven. Next time we'll lock him up somewhere."

"Next time," she corrected him, "we'll go to my place — if you don't mind sitting on the floor. I don't have any furniture yet. Only a bed," she added with a sidelong glance.

"How soon is next time?"

"After the medical conference. When I come back from Paris I'm leaving the Mooseville clinic. I'm tired of taking fishhooks out of tourists' backsides."

"What do you plan to do?"

"Join my father's office in Pickax."

"I'll be your first patient. Can you check cholesterol, heart, and all that?"

"You'll be surprised what I can do!" She threw him another of her provocative green-eyed glances.

Qwilleran escorted Melinda to her silver convertible parked discreetly in the garage — not a bad idea, as it turned out.

When she finally drove away, he walked back to the house with a buoyant step and found Koko waiting for him with a smug look of accomplishment.

"You're not as smart as you think you are," Qwilleran said to him, preening his moustache with satisfaction.

Early the next morning he walked downtown to

Amanda's studio to order a sofa. The crotchety designer was out on a house call, but a friendly young assistant produced some catalogues of contemporary furniture. Within five minutes Qwilleran had ordered a slouchy sofa in rust-colored suede, a brown lounge chair and ottoman, and some reading lamps — for his new studio.

"You have good taste," the assistant said, "and I've never seen a client make such speedy decisions. I'd love to see your carriage house when it's finished."

"And what is your name?" he asked.

"Francesca Brodie. My father knows you — by reputation, that is. He's the police chief. Aren't you sort of a detective?"

"I like to solve puzzles, that's all," Qwilleran said. "Did you ever know a Daisy Mull who worked here?"

"No, I've only been here four months."

For the next two days Qwilleran spent most of his time answering the letters that came shooting through the mail slot in great number, much to the delight of the Siamese. Koko personally delivered an envelope addressed in red ink, and he was not surprised that it came from a building in which they had recently lived. The letter was written by another tenant, a young woman who used to speak French to Koko and who was subject to problems with weight and problems with men. She wrote:

Dear Qwill,

Arch Riker gave me your address. Congratulations on striking oil! We miss you.

Want to hear my good news? I'm dating a chef now, and he's not married — or so he says. The bad news is that I've gained ten pounds. I'm still hacking copy at the ad agency, but I'd kill to get into the restaurant business. If you'd like to open a restaurant in Pickax, let me know. Have chef; will travel. Say bonjour to Koko.

Hixie Rice

Other letters arrived faster than Qwilleran could poke out answers on his old typewriter. The telephone rang constantly. And there were other interruptions, as when a young man in white coveralls suddenly appeared at the door of the library, carrying a six-pack of diet cola.

"Hi!" he said. "Mind if I put this in your fridge? This is a big job. Lots of spackling and patching and scraping, and some of the woodwork's bleeding."

He had the wholesome look of a Moose County native, raised on bushels of apples, milk right from the cow, vegetables from the garden, and unlimited fresh air.

"I assume you're a painter employed by Amanda Goodwinter," Qwilleran said.

"Yeah, I'm Steve. She's always telling people I'm slow, but I do good work. My grandfather worked on this house when the Old Lady was alive. He showed me how to paint without laps or drips or sags or pimples. Hey, do you really live in this joint? I live in a mobile home on my father-in-law's farm."

There were other reasons for Qwilleran's discontent. Mrs Cobb had not arrived. There was no sign of anyone to fix the doors. Melinda had left for Paris. And an exasperating melody kept running through his mind: *Daisy, Daisy*.

Then a schoolteacher he had met in Mooseville telephoned and said, "Hi, Qwill, this is Roger. How does it feel to be filthy rich?"

"Arduous, frustrating, and annoying — so far. But give me another week to get used to it. How's everything at the lake?"

"Oh, you know . . . lots of tourists and happy merchants."

"Is business good at your wife's shop?"

"Not bad, but she puts in long hours. Say, want to meet me for dinner somewhere tonight? Sharon's working late."

"Sure. Why don't you drive down here to the Bastille?" Qwilleran suggested. "I'll give you a conducted tour of the dungeons and pour you a drink. Then we can find a restaurant."

"Great! I'd like to see inside that rockpile. We can eat at the Hotel Booze."

"That's a new one to me."

"Oldest flophouse in the county. They have a twelve-ounce bacon cheeseburger with fries that's the greatest!"

Roger MacGillivray, whose Scottish name appealed to Qwilleran, arrived in the early evening. He was a young man with a clipped black beard and vigorous opinions, and he exclaimed about the size of the rooms, the number of windows, the height of the ceilings, and the extent of the property. "It'll cost an arm and a leg to maintain this place," he predicted. "Who's going to clean all those windows and dust all those books?"

"The landscape service alone costs more than I

earned at the *Daily Fluxion,*" Qwilleran informed him. "There's always a green truck in the driveway and a guy in a green jumpsuit riding around on a little green tractor."

He poured Scotch for his guest and white grape juice for himself, and they sat in the big wicker chairs in the solarium.

Roger stared at Qwilleran's stemmed glass. "What are you drinking?"

"Catawba grape juice. Koko likes it, so I bought a case of it."

"You really pamper that animal." Roger glanced around apprehensively. "Where is he? I'm not comfortable with cats."

Koko, hearing his name, sauntered into the solarium and positioned himself in Roger's view.

"He won't bother you," Qwilleran said. "He enjoys listening to our conversation, that's all. He likes the tone of your voice."

Koko moved a little closer.

"Who looks after these rubber plants, Qwill? They look healthier than I do."

"The green jumpsuit comes in and sticks a meter in the soil and takes a reading," Qwilleran said. "The whole horticultural scene is too esoteric for me. I've spent all my life in apartments and hotels."

"I think your gardener is Kevin Doone, a former student of mine. He goes to Princeton now and does gardening during summer vacation. You've got a pretty good-sized lot."

"Half a block wide and half a mile long, I estimate.

There's an orchard back there and an old barn that would make a good summer theater."

Roger gripped the arms of his chair. "Why is he looking at me like that?"

"Koko wants to be friends. Say something to him."

"Hello, Koko," Roger said in a weak voice.

The cat blinked his eyes shut and emitted a squeaky, nonthreatening "ik ik ik."

"He's smiling," Qwilleran said. "He likes you . . . How's your mother-in-law, Roger?"

"She's fine. She's gung ho about a new craft project now — designing things with a Moose County theme, for Sharon to sell in her shop. Pot holders and toys and stuff. The idea is to have the Dimsdale women make them by hand — sort of a cottage industry. She wanted to get a grant from the state, but there was too much red tape. Besides that, the people in Dimsdale don't want to work. Do you know that place?"

"I've seen the remains of the Dimsdale Mine," Qwilleran said, "and I've eaten at the decrepit diner at the intersection, but I thought it was mainly a ghost town."

"Officially Dimsdale doesn't exist, but there's a bunch of shanties back in the woods — squatters, you know. In fact, I think they're on Klingenschoen property, your property. You'd never believe it, Qwill, but a hundred years ago Dimsdale was a thriving town with hotels, a sawmill, housing for miners, stores, even a doctor."

"You know a lot about local history, Roger."

"I ought to! That's what I teach . . . Say, he's a good-looking animal, isn't he? Very well behaved."

"His real name is Kao K'o Kung. He was named after a thirteenth-century Chinese artist."

Knowing he was the topic of conversation, Koko casually ambled over to Roger's chairside.

"If you've never stroked a Siamese," Qwilleran said, "you don't know what fur is all about."

Cautiously Roger extended a hand and patted the silky fawn-colored back. "Good boy!" he said. "Good boy!"

The cat looked at Qwilleran, slowly closing one eye, and Qwilleran thought, Score another one for Koko.

The two men finished their drinks and then drove from the palatial splendor of the K mansion to the stolid ugliness of the Hotel Booze. It was a stone building three stories high, with the plain shoebox architecture typical of hotels in pioneer towns. A sign, almost as big as the hotel itself, advertised booze, rooms, and food.

"In this hotel," Roger said, "a miner could get a man-sized dinner and a bed on the floor for a quarter, using his boots for a pillow, or a sack of oats if he was lucky."

The dim lighting in the dining room camouflaged the dreary walls and ancient linoleum floor and worn plastic tables. Nevertheless, the room hummed with the talk of customers wearing feed caps and wolfing down burgers and beer.

Qwilleran tried three chairs before finding one with all its legs and rungs. "I'll have the Cholesterol Special," he told the waitress, a homey-looking woman in a faded housedress.

"Make it two, Thelma," said Roger.

The sandwich proved to be so enormous that she

served it with her thumb on top of the bun to hold it all together.

"We call her Thumbprint Thelma," Roger whispered.

Qwilleran had to admit that the burger was superior and the fries tasted like actual potatoes. "Okay, Roger, how about a history lesson to take my mind off the calories? Tell me about the abandoned mines around here."

"There were ten of them in the old days — all major operations. Shafts went a thousand feet deep, and the miners had to climb down on a *ladder*! After a long day underground, with water dripping all around, it took half an hour to climb back up to the surface."

"Like climbing a hundred-storey building! They must have been desperate for work."

"Most of them came from Europe — left their families behind — and hoped to send money home. But — what with payday binges at the saloon and buying on credit at the company store — they were always in hock."

Thelma brought coffee, and Roger — without much difficulty — persuaded Qwilleran to try the wild thimbleberry pie.

"Picked the berries myself this morning," the waitress said.

The men savored each forkful in the reverent silence that the pie merited and ordered second cups of coffee.

Qwilleran said, "I suppose the old saloons had gambling in the back room and girls upstairs."

"Right! And a bizarre sense of fun. When a customer drank too much and passed out, his pals carried him outside and nailed his boots to the wooden sidewalk. And there was always an old soak hanging around the saloon who would do anything for a drink. One of these characters used to eat poison ivy. Another would bite the head off a live chipmunk."

"This isn't the best dinner-table conversation I've ever heard, Roger."

"I'm telling it like it was! The K Saloon was notorious."

"Is that what you teach in your history classes?"

"Well, it grabs their attention. The kids eat it up!"

Qwilleran was silent for a moment before he asked, "Did you ever have a student by the name of Daisy Mull?"

"No, she dropped out before I started teaching, but my mother-in-law had her in art class. She said Daisy was the only Mull who would ever amount to anything — if she applied herself. She was kind of goofy."

Qwilleran told him about the graffiti — then about his plans for a studio over the garage — and then about his search for a housekeeper.

"How do you figure you'll adjust to a live-in housekeeper?" Roger asked him. "I suppose it's like having a wife, without the fringe benefits."

"Speak for yourself, Roger."

"Are you getting along okay with G&G?"

"So far, so good. Penelope is the one handling the estate. I haven't figured her out yet."

"She's the bright one in the family. What do you think of her brother?"

"Alexander hasn't been around much. He's gone to Washington again."

Roger lowered his voice. "There's a rumor he's got a

woman down there. If he's serious, it's big news. Alex has always been a confirmed bachelor."

"Is Penelope involved with anyone?"

"Why? Are you interested?"

"No thanks. I've got all I can handle at the moment."

"She never bothers with guys," Roger said. "Strictly careerist. Too bad. She's really got it together."

Qwilleran picked up the check and paid the cashier on the way out. She was a large woman in a patterned muumuu splashed with oversize black-eyed Susans. Qwilleran found himself whistling *Daisy, Daisy.*

Instantly the hubbub in the dining room dissolved into silence, and the cashier wagged a finger at Qwilleran. "That's a no-no." She pointed to a sign over the cash register: *No credit. No checks. No spitting. No whistling.*

"Sorry," Qwilleran said.

"It's bad luck," Roger explained. "It used to be considered unlucky to whistle in the mines, and the superstition stuck. There's no whistling in Pickax — by city ordinance."

CHAPTER SIX

He had never been much of a whistler, but as soon as Qwilleran learned that whistling was forbidden in Pickax he felt a compulsion to whistle. As he prepared the cats' breakfast he whistled an air from *The Mikado*, causing Koko to twist his ears inside out and run into the back entry hall. Yum Yum went slinking into the laundry room and crouched behind their commode.

The cats' commode was an oval roasting pan containing a layer of kitty gravel — an unorthodox but substantial piece of equipment that worked well. Their water dish was an Imari porcelain bowl that Qwilleran had found in the butler's pantry. Their food he arranged on a porcelain dinner plate with a wide blue and gold border — appropriate because the border matched the ineffable blue of Yum Yum's eyes, and because the gold-embellished crest bore a *K*.

Qwilleran put a plate of canned red salmon on the floor in the laundry room and called the cats. Yum Yum reported immediately, but there was no response from Koko.

"Drat him! He's gone up to the attic again," Qwilleran muttered. It was true. The door to the attic stairs stood ajar, and Koko was on the third floor, sharpening his claws on a roll of carpet.

Qwilleran made a lunge for him, but the cat eluded his grasp and bounded to the top of an Art Nouveau chifforobe, where he assumed a challenging posture. Then it was an insane chase around the dusty storeroom — Koko streaking over a General Grant bed, under a bowlegged Chinese table, around a barricade of steamer trunks, with Qwilleran breathing heavily in stubborn pursuit.

Koko finally allowed himself to be caught, while crouching defiantly on a cheap cardboard suitcase patterned to resemble tweed. Qwilleran's moustache sent him a signal: another item of significance! He grabbed an unprotesting cat in one hand and the suitcase in the other and descended to the kitchen, where Yum Yum was washing up after finishing the whole can of salmon.

Attached to the broken handle of the luggage there was a tag written in the perfect penmanship he had seen before: *Daisy Mull*. The contents had the same musty odor he remembered from opening her carton of winter clothing. This time the collection included sandals, T-shirts, cutoffs, a faded sundress, underpants dotted with red hearts, and the briefest of swimsuits.

Qwilleran could explain why the girl had abandoned her cold-weather gear, but why had she left her summer wearables as well? Perhaps she had lined up a situation that would provide an entirely new wardrobe — either a job or a generous patron. Perhaps a tourist from some other part of the country had come up here and staked her to a getaway — for better or worse. Qwilleran wished the poor girl well.

There were other items in the suitcase: a paper bag containing tasteless junk jewelry as well as one fourteen-karat gold bracelet, heavy enough to make one wonder. Had she stolen it? And if so, why had she left it behind? Another paper bag was stuffed with messy cosmetics and a toothbrush; she had left in a hurry!

There was one more surprise in the suitcase. In a shopping bag with the Lanspeak's Department Store logo Qwilleran found a pathetic assortment of baby clothes.

He sat down in a kitchen chair to think about it. Had she left town hurriedly to have an abortion? After starting a sentimental collection of bootees and tiny sweaters with rosebuds crocheted into the design, why had she decided to end her pregnancy? And what had happened to her? Why had she not returned? Did her family know her fate? Did they know her present whereabouts? Did she even have a family? If so, did they live in that shantytown near the old Dimsdale Mine site? Unanswered questions tormented Qwilleran, and he knew he would never stop probing this one until he had an answer.

His ruminations were interrupted by the sound of a vehicle in the service drive. Dropping the gold bracelet into his pocket, he stuffed the rest of Daisy's belongings back into the sad excuse for a suitcase — broken handle, torn lining, scuffed corners. Then he went outdoors to greet Mrs Cobb. Her van was filled to the roof with boxes of books, which he began to carry into the house.

She was happy to the point of tears. "I'm so thrilled, I don't know where to begin."

"Get yourself settled comfortably," he said. "Then make a list of what you need for the refrigerator and pantry. The cats are looking forward to your Swedish meatballs and deviled crab."

"What do you like to eat, Mr Qwilleran?"

"I eat everything — except parsnips and turnips. I'll take you out to lunch this noon, and then I have an appointment at my attorney's office."

The meeting that Penelope had scheduled included Mr Fitch from the bank and Mr Cooper, accountant for the estate. The banker was well tanned; Mr Cooper was ghastly pale in spite of the sunshine that was parching Moose County. Mr Fitch graciously congratulated Qwilleran on his proposal to start an eleemosynary foundation. He also inquired if Qwilleran golfed.

"I'm afraid I'm a Moose County anomaly," was the answer. "Non-golfing, non-fishing, non-hunting."

"We'll have to do something about that," said the banker cordially. "I'd like to sponsor you for the country club."

The first order of business concerned the opening of a drawing account at the bank. Then Penelope suggested to Qwilleran that he start sifting through any documents he might find in the house. "It would be wise," she said, "to acquaint yourself with insurance coverage, taxes, household inventories, and the like before turning them over to our office."

He squirmed uncomfortably. He despised that kind of paperwork.

"Is everything progressing smoothly?" she asked, smiling and dimpling.

"The housekeeper arrived this morning," he said, "and she agrees we should have some day help."

"I recommend Mrs Fulgrove. She works for us a few days a week and is very thorough. Has Birch Trevelyan made contact with you?"

"Never showed up. All the doors need attention, and we definitely need a lock on the back door."

"That Birch is a lazy dog," said the banker. "You have to catch him at one of the coffee shops and twist his arm."

Penelope threw Mr Fitch a reproving glance. "I'll handle it, Nigel. I think I can put a little diplomatic pressure on the man . . . Do you have any questions, Mr Qwilleran?"

"When does the city council meet? Sitting in on a meeting is a good way to get acquainted with a new community. Mrs Cobb might like to go, too."

"In that case," Penelope said quickly, "I'll take the lady as my guest. It wouldn't be appropriate for you to escort her."

"Oh, come on, Penny," said the banker with a half laugh, and she threw him one of her sharp glances.

Turning to the silent accountant, she asked, "Do you have anything to add, Mr Cooper?"

"Good records," he said. "It's important to have good records. Do you keep good records, Mr Qwilleran?"

Qwilleran had visions of more paperwork. "Records of what?"

"Personal income, expenditures, deductions. Be sure

to keep receipts, vouchers, bank statements, and such."

Qwilleran nodded. The accountant had given him an idea. After the meeting he drew the man aside. "Do you have the records of domestic help at the Klingenschoen house, Mr Cooper? I'd like to know the dates of employment for one Daisy Mull."

"It's all in the computer," the accountant said. "I'll have my secretary phone you with the information."

In the ensuing days Qwilleran enjoyed the housekeeper's home cooking, answered letters, and bought new tires for the bicycle in the garage. He also telephoned the young managing editor of the *Picayune*. "When are you going to introduce me to coffee shop society, Junior? You promised."

"Any time. Where do you want to go? The best place is the Dimsdale Diner."

"I had lunch there once. I call it the Dismal Diner."

"You're not kidding either. I'll pick you up tomorrow morning at ten. Wear a feed cap," the editor advised, "and you'd better practice drinking coffee with a spoon in the cup."

Although Junior Goodwinter looked like a high school sophomore and always wore running shoes and a Pickax varsity letter, he had graduated from journalism school before going to work for his father's newspaper. They drove to the diner in his red Jaguar, the editor in a baseball cap and Qwilleran in a bright orange hunting cap.

"Junior, this county has the world's worst drivers," he said. "They straddle the centerline; they make turns from the wrong lane; they don't even know what turn signals are for. How do they get away with it?"

"We're more casual up here," Junior explained. "You people Down Below are all conformists, but we don't like anybody telling us what to do."

They parked in the dusty lot at the diner, among a fleet of vans and pickup trucks and one flashy motorcycle.

The Dismal Diner was an old railroad freight car that had been equipped with permanently dirty windows. The tables and chairs might have been cast-offs from the Hotel Booze when it redecorated in 1911. For the coffee hour, customers pushed tables together to seat clubby groups of eight or ten — all men wearing feed caps. They helped themselves to coffee and doughnuts on the counter and paid their money to a silent, emaciated man in a cook's apron. Cigarette smoke blurred the atmosphere. The babble of voices and raucous laughter was deafening.

Qwilleran and Junior, sitting at a side table, caught fragments of conversation:

"Never saw nothin' like what they put on TV these days."

"How's your dad's arthritis, Joe?"

"Man, don't try to tell me they're not livin' together."

"We need rain."

"The woman he's goin' with — they say she's a lawyer."

"Ever hear the one about the little city kid who had to draw a picture of a cow?"

Qwilleran leaned across the table. "Who are these guys?"

Junior scanned the group. "Farmers. Commercial fishermen. A branch bank manager. A guy who builds pole barns. One of them sells farm equipment; he's loaded. One of them cleans septic tanks."

Pipe smoke and the aroma of a cigar were added to the tobacco haze. Snatches of conversation were interwoven like a tapestry.

"Durned if I didn't fix my tractor with a piece of wire. Saved a coupla hundred, easy."

"Always wanted to go to Vegas, but my old lady, she says no."

"Forget handguns. I like a rifle for deer."

"My kid caught a bushel of perch at Purple Point in half an hour."

"We all know he's got his hand in the till. Never got caught, that's all."

"Here's Terry!" several voices shouted, and heads turned toward the dirty windows.

One customer rushed out the door. Picking up a wooden palette, he slanted it across the steps to make a ramp. Then a man in a feed cap, who had eased out of a low-slung car into a folding wheelchair, waited until he was pushed up the ramp into the diner.

"Dairy farmer," Junior whispered. "Bad accident a few years ago. Tractor rollover . . . Milks a hundred Holsteins an hour in a computerized milking parlor. Five hundred gallons a day. Eighteen tons of manure a year."

The talk went on — about taxes, the commodities market, and animal waste management systems. There was plenty of laughter — chesty guffaws, explosive roars, cackling and bleating. "Baa-a-a" laughed a customer behind Qwilleran.

"We all know who she's makin' eyes at, don't we? Baa-a-a!"

"Ed's new barn cost three quarters of a million."

"They sent him to college and dammit if he didn't get on dope."

"That which is crooked cannot be made straight, according to Ecclesiastes One-fifteen."

"Man, he'll never get married. He's got it too good. Baa-a-a!"

"We need rain bad."

"If he brings that woman here, there's gonna be hell to pay."

A sign over the doughnut tray read: "Cows may come and cows may go, but the bull in here goes on forever."

"I believe it," Qwilleran said. "This is a gossip factory."

"Nah," Junior said. "The guys just shoot the breeze."

Toward eleven o'clock customers began to straggle out, and a man with a cigar stopped to give Junior a friendly punch in the ribs. He had a big build and arrogant swagger, and he bleated like a sheep. He rode off on the flashy motorcycle in a blast of noise and flying gravel.

"Who's that?" Qwilleran asked.

"Birch Tree," Junior said. "It's really Trevelyan, an old family name in Moose County. His brother's name is Spruce, and he has two sisters, Maple and Evergreen. I told you we're individualists up here."

"That's the guy who's supposed to do our repairs, but he's taking his own sweet time."

"He's good, but he hates to work. Hikes his prices so people won't hire him. Always has plenty of dough, though. He's part owner of this diner, but that would never make anyone rich."

"Unless they're selling something besides food," Qwilleran said.

On the way back to Pickax he asked if women ever came to the coffee hour.

"Naw, they have their own gossip sessions with tea and cookies . . . Want to hear the eleven o'clock news?" He turned on the car radio.

Ever since arriving in Moose County Qwilleran had marveled at the WPKX news coverage. The local announcers had a style that he called Instant Paraphrase.

The newscaster was saying, ". . . lost control of his vehicle when a deer ran across the highway, causing the car to enter a ditch and sending the driver to the Pickax Hospital, where he was treated and released. A hospital spokesperson said the patient was treated for minor injuries and released.

"In sports, the Pickax Miners walloped the Mooseville Mosquitoes thirteen to twelve, winning the county pennant and a chance at the play-offs. According to Coach Russell, the pennant gives the miners a chance to show their stuff in the regional play-offs."

Suddenly Junior's beeper sounded, and a siren at City Hall started to wail. "There's a fire," he said. "Mind if I drop you at the light? See you later."

His red Jaguar varoomed toward the fire hall, and Qwilleran walked the few remaining blocks. On every side he was hailed by strangers who seemed happy to see him and who used the friendly but respectful initial customary in Pickax.

"Hi, Mr Q."

"Morning, Mr Q."

"Nice day, Mr Q."

Mrs Cobb greeted him with a promise of meatloaf sandwiches for lunch. "And there's a message from Mr Cooper's office. The person you inquired about terminated her employment five years ago on July seventh. She started April third of that year. Also, a very strange woman walked in and said she'd been hired to clean three days a week. She's upstairs now, doing the bedrooms. And another thing, Mr Qwilleran — I found some personal correspondence in my desk upstairs, and I thought you should sort it out. It's on your desk in the library."

The correspondence filled a corrugated carton, and perched on top of the conglomeration of papers was Koko, sound asleep with his tail curled lovingly around his nose. Either the cat was developing a mail fetish, or he knew the carton had once contained a shipment of canned tuna.

Qwilleran removed the sleeping animal and tackled the old Klingenschoen correspondence. There was no order or sense to the collection, and nothing of historic or financial importance. Mail that should have been thrown into a waste-basket had been pigeon-holed in a desk. A letter from a friend, dated 1921, had been filed with a solicitation for a recent Boy Scout drive.

What caught Qwilleran's attention was a government

postal card with two punctures in one corner, looking suspiciously like the mark of feline fangs.

The message read:

"Writing on bus. Sorry didn't say goodbye. Got job in Florida — very sudden. Got a lift far as Cleveland. Throw out all my things. Don't need anything. Good job — good pay."

It was signed with the name that had been haunting Qwilleran for the last ten days, and it was dated July 11, five years before. Curiously enough, there was a Maryland postmark. Why the girl was traveling from Cleveland to Florida by way of Maryland was not clear. Qwilleran also noted that the handwriting bore no resemblance to the precise penmanship on Daisy's luggage tags.

He ripped the tag from the suitcase in the kitchen and went in search of Mrs Fulgrove. He found her in the Empire suite, furiously attacking a marble-topped, sphinx-legged table with her soft cloths and mysterious potions.

"This place was let go somethin' terrible," she said, "which don't surprise me, seein' as how the Old Lady didn't have no decent help for five years, but I'm doin' my best to put things to rights, and it ain't easy when you're my age and pestered with a bad shoulder, which I wouldn't wish it on my worst enemy."

Qwilleran complimented her on her industry and principles and showed her the luggage tag. "Do you know anything about this?"

"Course I do, it's my own writin', and nobody writes proper anymore, but the nuns taught us how to write so's anybody could read it, and when the Old Lady told me to put that girl's things in the attic, I marked 'em so's there'd be no mistake."

"Why did the Old Lady keep Daisy's clothing, Mrs Fulgrove? Was the girl expected to return?"

"Heaven knows what the Old Lady took it in her head to do. She never throwed nothin' away, and when she told me to pack it all in the attic, I packed it in the attic and no questions asked."

Qwilleran disengaged himself from the conference and let Mrs Fulgrove return to her brass polish and marble restorer and English wax. He himself went back to answering letters. The afternoon delivery brought another avalanche spilling into the vestibule, to be distributed by the two self-appointed mail clerks. Koko delivered a card announcing a new seafood restaurant, as well as a letter from Roger's mother-in-law. She wrote:

Dear Qwill,

Are you enjoying your new lifestyle? Don't forget you're only thirty miles from Mooseville. Drop in some afternoon. I've been picking wild blueberries for pies.

Mildred Hanstable

She had been Qwilleran's neighbor at the beach, and he remembered her as a generous-hearted woman who loved people. He seized the phone and immediately accepted the invitation — not only because she made superb pies but because she had been Daisy Mull's art teacher.

Driving up to the shore the next afternoon he sensed a difference in the environment as he approached the lake — not only the lushness of vegetation and freshness of breeze but a general air of relaxation and well-being. It was the magic that lured tourists to Mooseville.

The Hanstable summer cottage overlooked the lake, and an umbrella table was set up for the repast.

"Mildred, your blueberry pie is perfection," Qwilleran said. "Not too gelatinous, not too viscous, not too liquescent."

She laughed with pleasure. "Don't forget I teach home ec as well as art. In our school district we have to be versatile, like coaching girls' volleyball and directing the senior play."

"Do you remember a student named Daisy Mull?" he asked.

"Do I ever! I had great hopes for Daisy. Why do you ask?"

"She worked for the Klingenschoens a while back, and I found some of her artwork."

"Daisy had talent. That's why I was so disappointed when she didn't continue. It's unusual for that kind of talent to surface in Moose County. The focus is on sports, raising families, and watching TV. Daisy dropped out of school and eventually left town."

"Where did she go?"

"I don't know. She never kept in touch, to my knowledge — not even with her mother, although that's easy to understand. What kind of artwork did you find?"

Qwilleran described the murals.

"I'd love to see them," Mildred said. "In fact I'd like to see the whole house, if you wouldn't mind. Roger says it's a showplace."

"I think we can arrange that . . . Didn't Daisy get along with her mother?"

"Mrs Mull has a drinking problem, and it's hard for a young girl to cope with an alcoholic parent . . . Please help yourself to the pie, Qwill."

He declined a third helping, reminding himself that Mrs Cobb was planning lamb stew with dumplings for dinner, with her famous coconut cake for dessert.

He drew a postal card from his pocket. "I found this at the house, dated five years ago. Daisy was on her way to Florida."

Mildred looked at the address side of the card, frowning a little. Then she turned it over and read the message twice. She shook her head. "Qwill, this is definitely not Daisy's handwriting."

CHAPTER SEVEN

Qwilleran sat in a deck chair on the Hanstable terrace overlooking the lake. Clouds scudded across the blue sky and waves lapped the beach, but his mind was elsewhere. Why would anyone forge a communication to Daisy's employer? He could make a guess or two, but he needed more information.

"How do you know," he asked his hostess, "that this card wasn't written by Daisy?"

"It's not her handwriting or her spelling," Mildred said with assurance. "She'd never put a *w* in 'writing' or an *e* in 'goodbye' or an apostrophe in anything. She could draw, but she couldn't spell."

"You knew her very well?"

"Let me tell you something, Qwill. For a teacher — a *real* teacher — the biggest reward is to discover raw material and nurture it and watch it develop. I worked hard with Daisy — tried to raise her sights. I knew she could get a scholarship and go into commercial art. It would have been a giant step forward for anyone with the name of Mull. She had invented an individual style of handwriting — hard to read but pleasing to the eye — so I know that *no way* did she write that postcard."

"Any idea who might have written it?"

"Not the faintest. Why on earth would anyone . . ."

Qwilleran said, "Was there any reason why she might want people in Pickax to *think* she had gone to Florida? Was she afraid of someone here? Afraid of being followed and brought back? Were the police looking for her? Had she stolen something? She may have gone out west but arranged for someone else to mail the card in Maryland. Was she clever enough to figure that out? Did she have an accomplice?"

Mildred looked distressed as well as bewildered. "She took a rather pricey object from the decorating studio, but Amanda didn't prosecute. Honestly, I can't imagine Daisy being involved in a serious theft."

"What kind of guys did she go around with?"

"Not the most respectable, I'm afraid. She started . . . *hanging out* after she left school."

"Would her mother know her friends?"

"I suspect her mother would neither know nor care."

"I'd like to talk with that woman."

"It might not be easy. The Mulls are suspicious of strangers, and Della isn't sober very often. I could try to see her when I go to Dimsdale to check on my craft workers. Della does nice knitting and crochet, and she could make items for Sharon's shop, but she can't get herself together."

"You could tell her I've found her daughter's belongings," Qwilleran said, "including a valuable piece of gold jewelry. Stress 'valuable,' and see how she reacts. Ask if I might deliver Daisy's luggage to her."

"Did she really have some good jewelry?" Mildred asked.

"It was in her suitcase in the attic. The question is: why did she leave it behind? She disappeared in the month of July and left both summer and winter clothing, including her toothbrush and . . . Did you know she was pregnant?"

"I'm not surprised," Mildred said sadly. "She never got any love at home. How do you know she was pregnant?"

"She'd been buying baby clothes from Lanspeak's — that is, buying or shoplifting. She left those behind, too. My first hunch was that she was running away to have an abortion."

"She could have had a miscarriage. That can unhinge a woman, and Daisy wasn't the most stable girl in the world — or the healthiest."

"To tell you the truth, Mildred," said Qwilleran, "I'm getting some unsavory vibrations about this case. But I can't say any more — just yet."

Driving back to Pickax he made a detour at the Dimsdale intersection. Just as Roger had said, a dirt road led back into the woods, and among the trees were flat-roofed shacks and old travel trailers. The number of small outhouses suggested a lack of plumbing in this shantytown. Junk was scattered everywhere: bedsprings, an old refrigerator without a door, fragments of farm machinery, rusted-out cars without wheels. The only vehicles that looked operative were trucks in the last stages of dilapidation. Here and there a dusty vegetable garden was struggling to survive in a clearing. Gray washing hung on sagging clotheslines. Flocks of small children played among the rubbish, shrieking and tumbling and chasing chickens.

Comparing the scene with his own lavish residence, Qwilleran cringed — and put the Dimsdale squatters on his mental list for the K Foundation: decent housing, skill training, meaningful jobs, something like that.

At the K mansion he was surprised to see a motorcycle parked at the back door. The service drive was usually occupied by a pickup or two. The green jumpsuit was constantly mowing, edging, watering, spraying and pruning, and Amanda's crew was always coming and going on obscure missions. This afternoon there was a black motorcycle — long in the wheelbase, wide in the tank, voluptuous as to fairings, and loaded with chrome.

Qwilleran stepped into the entry hall and heard voices: "Whaddaya see, Iris baby? Gimme the bad news."

"Your palm is very good, very easy to read. I see a long lifeline and — oh my! — many love affairs."

"Baa-a-a-a!"

There was no mistaking the laugh or the motorcycle.

In the kitchen the scene was casual, to say the least. Birch Trevelyan in his field boots and feed cap sprawled in a chair at the kitchen table, a T-shirt stretched across his beefy chest and a leather jacket with cutoff sleeves hanging on a doorknob. Mrs Cobb, apparently dazzled by this macho glamour, was holding his hand and stroking the palm. Koko was monitoring the situation from the top of the refrigerator, not without alarm. Yum Yum was under the table sniffing the man's boots. And on the table were the remains of the three-layer, cream-filled coconut cake that Mrs Cobb had baked for Qwilleran's evening meal.

She jumped to her feet, looking flushed and guilty. "Oh, there you are, Mr Qwilleran. This is Birch Tree. He's going to solve all our repair problems."

"Howdy," said Birch in the coffee-shop style, loud and easy. "Pull up a chair. Have some cake. Baa-a-a!" His mismatched eyes — one brown, one hazel — had an evil glint, but he had a disarming grin showing big square teeth.

Qwilleran accepted a chair that Birch shoved in his direction and said, "That's some classy animal you've got tethered out there."

"Yeah, it's a mean rig. Y'oughta get one. You can hit a hundred-fifty in sixth on the airport road, if it's clear. Ten miles of straight, there. Ittibittiwassee — you get four straight but you rev up to ten grand and it's all over."

Tactfully Qwilleran slipped into the topic of primary interest. "There's something wrong with the doors in this house, Birch. They don't latch properly. Even the cat can open them."

"Lotta muscle in one of them small packages," Birch said with authority.

"We've got about twenty doors that won't stay shut. What can be done?"

The expert tucked his thumbs in his belt, rocked his chair on two legs, and nodded wisely. "Old house. Building settles. Doorframes get out of whack. Doors shrink. I can fix 'em, but it'll cost ya."

For a man who hated to work, he seemed most

agreeable. New lock for the back door? “Easy!” Twenty doors refitted? “Piece o’ cake!”

He said he would start the next morning — early. Qwilleran surmised that Mrs Cobb had bribed him with a promise of huckleberry pancakes and sausages.

After Birch had roared away on his motorcycle, the housekeeper said, “Isn’t that a wonderful machine?”

Qwilleran grunted noncommittally. “How is he going to transport tools with that thing?”

“Oh, he told me he has a couple of trucks, and an ORV, and one of those big campers. He likes wheels. He wants to take me for a ride on the motorbike. What do you think?”

Qwilleran exhaled audibly into his moustache. “Don’t rush into anything with that guy. I think he’s an opportunist.”

“He seems very nice. When I told him that smoke was harmful to antiques, he chucked his cigar without a word. And he *loved* my coconut cake.”

“That’s obvious. He ate most of it.”

“Even little Yum Yum liked him. Did you see her sniffing his boots?”

“Either he’d been walking around a barnyard or she was looking for a shoelace to untie. It wasn’t necessarily a character endorsement . . . By the way, have you noticed Koko sitting on the main staircase a lot?”

She nodded. “That’s his favorite perch, except for the refrigerator.”

“The strange thing is that he always sits on the *third stair*. I don’t understand why.”

The housekeeper looked warily at Qwilleran. “I have

something strange to report, too, but I'm afraid you'll laugh at me."

"Mrs Cobb, I always take you seriously."

"Well, you remember I mentioned ghosts when I came here. I was only kidding, sort of, but now I'm beginning to think this house is haunted — not that I'm afraid, you understand."

"How did you get that idea?"

"Well, sometimes when I come into the kitchen at night I see a white blur out of the corner of my eye, but when I turn to look, it's gone."

"I'm always seeing white blurs, Mrs Cobb. One's called Koko and the other's called Yum Yum."

"But things also move around mysteriously — mostly in the kitchen. Twice it was the kitchen wastebasket, right in the middle of the floor. Last night that old suitcase was shoved across the doorway. Do you know anything about the people who lived here, Mr Qwilleran? Were there any unexplained deaths? I don't know whether you really believe in ghosts."

"These days I'll believe anything."

"It's dangerous. I almost fell over the suitcase in the dark. What's it doing here? It seems to be full of musty clothes."

"I'll put it in the broom closet — get it out of the way. And you must promise to turn on lights when you come in here after dark."

"I guess I'm used to saving electricity."

"Forget about that. The estate owns a big chunk of the electric company. And please don't walk around without your glasses, Mrs Cobb. How's your eye problem these days?"

She held up two crossed fingers. "I still see the eye doctor twice a year."

"Is everything else working out all right? Any questions?"

"Well, I took some cookies over to the painter in the garage — he's a nice young man — and he showed me the huge daisies all over the walls. Who painted those?"

"A girl named Daisy, by a strange coincidence. She used to work here. I hope you're not planning to paint irises all over the kitchen."

"Oh, Mr Qwilleran," she laughed.

"Have you started to catalogue the collection?"

"Yes, and I'm terribly excited. There's a silver vault in the basement with some eight-branch silver candelabra about three feet high. The butler's pantry has china to serve twenty-four, and the linen closet has damask and Madeira banquet cloths like you wouldn't believe! You ought to give a big dinner party, Mr Qwilleran. I'd be glad to cook for it."

"Good idea," he said, "but don't try to do too much. Save some time for yourself. You might want to join the Historical Society, and when you're ready to take on appraisal jobs we'll run an ad in the *Picayune* — even get you some publicity on WPKX."

"Oh, that would be wonderful!"

"And how would you like to attend a city council meeting? I intend to go, and the attorney suggested you might enjoy it, too."

"Wasn't that sweet of her! Yes, I'd love to go," Mrs Cobb said, her eyes shining. "We had so much trouble with bureaucrats in the city; I'd like to see how a small town operates."

"Okay, it's a date. Now I'm going to take a bike ride before dinner."

"Mr Qwilleran," the housekeeper said hesitantly, "it's none of my business, but I'd like to say something if it won't offend you."

"Fire away!"

"I wish you'd get a new bicycle. That old one is such a rattletrap! It's not safe."

"The bike's perfectly safe, Mrs Cobb. I've cleaned it and oiled it and bought new tires. It has a few squeaks, but it's good enough for my purposes."

"But there are so many trucks, and they travel so fast! They could blow you right off the road."

"I do most of my biking on country roads, where there's very little traffic. Don't worry."

The housekeeper set her mouth primly. "But it doesn't *look right* for a man in your position to be riding a — riding a piece of junk, if you'll pardon the expression."

"And if you'll pardon my saying so, Mrs Cobb, you're beginning to sound like Penelope Goodwinter. Those eight-branch candelabra have gone to your head."

She smiled sheepishly.

"While I'm gone," he said, "Miss Goodwinter might call to say when she's picking us up for the council meeting. Also, a Mrs Hanstable might phone. She wants a tour of the house. Tell her that any time tomorrow will be okay. I'm going to start charging twenty bucks for these tours."

"Oh, Mr Qwilleran, you must be kidding."

In order to bike on country roads he had to negotiate four blocks of downtown traffic, five blocks of old residential streets, and then six blocks of suburbia abounding in prefabricated ranch houses, children, plastic tricycles, dogs, and barbecue smoke. After that came the lonely serenity of open country — pastureland, old mine sites, patches of woods, and an occasional farmhouse with a bicycle-chasing dog.

As he pedaled along the four straight miles on Ittibittiwassee Road he thought of many things: lamb stew and dumplings for dinner . . . Melinda coming home soon . . . the loungy sofa he had ordered . . . Arch Riker's pending visit . . . a tick-tick-tick in the rear wheel . . . a dinner party with three-foot silver candelabra . . . poor Mrs Cobb, too long a widow . . . a new grinding noise in the sprocket . . . *Daisy, Daisy* . . . the police chief with a good Scottish name . . . cream-filled coconut cake.

"The nerve of that guy!" he said aloud, and a lonely cow on the side of the road turned her head to look at him benignly.

Nerve was Birch Tree's outstanding trait. Early the next morning he arrived with a truckful of tools, an appetite for breakfast, and a portable radio. Qwilleran was half awake when a blast of noise catapulted him from his bed. Raucous music was augmented by a concert of caterwauling.

Grabbing his old plaid robe, he bolted downstairs and

found the maintenance man happily at work on a kitchen door. Yum Yum was screeching like the siren at City Hall, and Koko was exercising his full range of seven octaves as the music pulsed out of a radio with satellite speakers and a control panel like a video game.

"Cut the volume!" Qwilleran shouted. "It's hurting their ears!"

"Throw 'em a fish head and they'll shut up," Birch yelled. "Baa-a-a-a!"

Qwilleran made a dive for the controls. "If you want to know, Birch, that blaster hurts *my* ears, too."

Mrs Cobb beckoned him into the laundry room. "Let's not discourage him," she whispered. "He's touchy, and we want to keep him on the job."

For the next few days Birch Tree was always underfoot, modifying the volume of his radio in proportion to Mrs Cobb's supply of food, compliments, and beer. The whine of power tools turned the cats' ears inside out, but Qwilleran learned to accept the chaos as a positive indication of progress.

On the afternoon that Mildred Hanstable came to see the house, the tour started in the garage, where the slow-motion painter was spreading Mojave beige in Qwilleran's future studio. They picked their way among buckets, ladders, and drop cloths to reach Daisy's apartment.

At the sight of it the art teacher caught her breath. "It's remarkable! A *tour de force*! A poor girl's Sistine Chapel!" Tears came to her eyes. "That sad little creature! I wonder if she'll ever return."

Qwilleran fingered his moustache uncertainly.

"Frankly, I'm beginning to doubt that Daisy's alive."

"What are you trying to tell me, Qwill?"

"We don't know if she ever really left town, do we?"

"Do you suspect something . . . *awful*?"

"I don't know. It's just a hunch, but it's a strong one." How could he tell her about the tremor on his upper lip and the tune that kept running through his mind? "Let's go to the house, Mildred, and you can tell me what Daisy's mother said."

As they turned to leave the apartment the congenial Steve was standing in the doorway, holding a paint roller and shaking his head. "I'd hate to hafta paint this room. Did she do it all by herself? Crazy Daisy! That's what we called her in school."

"Just go back and push that roller, Speedo," Qwilleran said with a fraternal punch on the shoulder. "No laps, no sags, no drips, no pimples."

In the main house he conducted Mildred through the rooms with the finesse of a professional guide. "Opposite the fireplace you see a *pietra dura* cabinet, late seventeenth century. The Regency desk is laburnum with kingswood banding." Mrs Cobb was training him well.

"All this art! All this splendor!" Mildred exclaimed. "You don't expect it in Moose County."

"Very few people knew what this house contained," Qwilleran said. "The Klingenschoens never entertained, although they owned a boxcarful of china and silver . . . Would you like a drink?"

"Do you have any fruit juice?"

He served white grape juice from Koko's private stock,

and they sat in the solarium, where Mildred critiqued the marbled sculptures. It was mercifully quiet, except for an occasional "Baa-a-a!" Birch had turned off his radio and was having a beer with Mrs Cobb in the kitchen. Either the housekeeper was totally smitten, or she was a master strategist. The work was being done, and it was being done well.

"And now," Qwilleran said to Mildred, "tell me about Mrs Mull."

"She was fairly sober and quite agreeable. I gave her your message, and when I mentioned the gold jewelry she perked up noticeably."

"Did she have any news of her daughter?"

"None, but here's something interesting. She too received a postcard shortly after Daisy left. Something like 'Going to Florida . . . never coming back . . . forget about me . . . you never loved me.' Della was quite bitter about it."

"Did you see the card?"

"She hadn't kept it. And naturally she didn't remember the postmark or the handwriting or the date. That was five years ago, and she's been in a fog most of the time."

Qwilleran said, "I went to the police station and met Chief Brodie. Pleasant guy, very cooperative. Daisy had no record — no arrests, no complaints. I gave him the date when she left, but there was no report to Missing Persons."

"I'm relieved to know she has a clean slate," Mildred said. "She wasn't a *bad* girl, but the odds were against her. She used to come to school in rags. I kept some of Sharon's old clothes in the art room, and I'd make

Daisy put them on. Yesterday I looked up some of the old yearbooks. She was a sophomore when she left school, but her picture wasn't in the book. Couldn't afford to have a photo taken, I guess. There was a comment about each student, and for Daisy they said she'd marry a rich husband. I don't know whether they were being kind or cruel."

"I think I'll visit Della Mull tomorrow while she's in a good mood."

"Good. She lives in an old trailer with a big daisy painted on the door."

"Excuse me a minute," Qwilleran said. "I want to show you something." He went to the broom closet and returned with the baby clothes in a Lanspeak's shopping bag.

Mildred examined them thoughtfully.

"These aren't from Lanspeak's. They're handmade. It looks like Della's work."

"Then she knew Daisy was pregnant, didn't she? We may be getting somewhere. I'll know better tomorrow."

The next morning Qwilleran overheard a conversation that gave him an idea. Birch was again on the job, snacking with Mrs Cobb in the kitchen and describing the culinary delights of the Dimsdale Diner: corned beef and cabbage on special every Tuesday; foot-longs with chili every Wednesday. Qwilleran decided to take Della Mull to lunch. Women, he found, liked to be lunched. They became friendly and talkative. To Della, the Dismal Diner would be *haute cuisine*.

With the gold bracelet in a buttoned pocket, and with

Daisy's suitcase and carton of clothing in the trunk of his car, he started for Dimsdale shortly before noon. Halfway there he turned on the twelve o'clock newscast from WPKX: ". . . and you'll save dollars on top quality at Lanspeak's. Now for the headlines . . . The mayor of Pickax has assured local merchants that the downtown business district will have a new municipal parking lot before snow flies. In a speech before the Chamber of Commerce, Mayor Blythe said downtown would definitely have a new parking lot before snow flies.

"A Pickax restaurant has announced an expansion project that will increase seating capacity by fifty percent and create seven new jobs. Otto Geb, the proprietor of Otto's Tasty Eats, told WPKX that the new addition will serve fifty percent more customers and add seven employees to the payroll.

"A Dimsdale woman was found dead in her trailer home early this morning, a victim of accidental substance abuse. The body of Della Mull, forty-four, was found by a neighbor seeking to borrow a cigarette. The coroner's office ascribed death to alcohol and pills. According to Dr Barry Wimms, the ingestion of alcohol and pills was the cause of death.

"And now a friendly word from the folks at Lanspeak's."

CHAPTER EIGHT

"When are we going to have your memorable macaroni?" Qwilleran asked Mrs Cobb as they waited for Penelope Goodwinter to pick them up.

"As soon as I find some good nippy cheese. It has to be aged cheddar, you know," the housekeeper said. "By the way, I forgot to tell you — a woman phoned you and wants to come to see you. I told her to call back tomorrow. It's about Daisy, she said."

"Did you get her name?"

"It sounded like 'Tiffany Trotter,' but I'm not sure. She sounded young."

Mrs Cobb was wearing her no-iron pink pantsuit, and Qwilleran had thrown his wash-and-wear summer blazer over a club shirt. When the attorney drove up in her tan BMW, she was wearing a crisp linen suit in pin stripe mauve with a mauve silk shirt and mauve pearls. In a cordial but authoritative tone, Penelope instructed Mrs Cobb to sit in the back seat.

"My brother has returned," she told Qwilleran, "and we are discussing a plan of organization for the Klingenschoen Foundation. Everyone endorses the idea heartily. I have never seen such unanimity in this city. Usually there are several warring factions, even if the issue is only flowerboxes on Main Street."

The City Hall was a turreted stone edifice of medieval inspiration, lacking only a drawbridge and moat. With its parking lot, fire hall, police station, and ambulance garage, it occupied an entire city block, just off Main Street.

In the council chamber Mayor Blythe and the council members were assembling at a long table on a dais, and they included — to Qwilleran's surprise — two persons he knew: Amanda Goodwinter with her built-in scowl and Mr Cooper with his perpetually worried expression. Ten rows of chairs for the general public were already filled, except for three reserved seats in the front row. Penelope took care to seat herself between Qwilleran and his housekeeper.

The mayor's gavel rapped the table, and he intoned, "All rise for the Pledge of Allegiance."

Chairs were scraping the floor and the audience was struggling to its collective feet when a loud voice in the back of the room called out, "I object!"

Mrs Cobb gasped audibly. The audience groaned and sat down again. Council members fell back into their chairs with assorted grimaces of impatience, exasperation, and resignation. Looking around for the source of the disturbance, Qwilleran spotted a belligerent-looking middle-aged man with an outdated crew cut, standing and waiting to be recognized by the chair.

With stoic calm the mayor said, "Will you please state your objection, Mr Hackpole?"

"That's not the official flag of these United States," the man announced in a booming voice. "It's got forty-eight stars, and the federal government retired that piece of cloth in 1959."

The audience uttered another groan, and individuals shouted, "Who's counting? . . . Sit down!"

"Order!" Mayor Blythe banged the gavel. "Mr Hackpole, this flag has been saluted in this chamber for more than a quarter of a century without offending the tax-payers of Pickax or the federal government or the residents of Hawaii and Alaska."

"It's a violation of the flag code," insisted the objector. "What's right is right. What's wrong is wrong."

An elderly councilwoman said in a sweetly reasonable voice, "Many of us remember fondly that this flag was presented to the city of Pickax by the late Miss Klingenschoen, and it would be a mark of disrespect to remove it so soon after her untimely death."

"Hear! Hear!" was the response from the audience.

The somber accountant said, "This is an expensive flag. We couldn't afford to replace it with anything of like quality in today's market."

Scowling over her glasses, Amanda Goodwinter added, "It would have to be custom-made. This flag is one hundred percent virgin wool, lined with silk — very unusual. The stripes are individually stitched, and the stars are embroidered on the blue field. It was ordered through my studio."

"Don't forget the gold fringe," piped up a tremulous

voice from the end of the table. "You don't see many flags with gold fringe." The speaker was an old man so small that he virtually disappeared behind the council table.

A councilman of enormous girth, who occupied two armless chairs placed side by side, said, "Looks to me like the flag's got some moth holes in it."

"The holes could be darned," said the elderly woman sweetly. "I would do it myself if my eyesight were better."

"Darning is ridiculous," said Amanda with her usual bluntness. "Professional reweaving — that's what you need. But we'd have to send it Down Below, and we wouldn't get it back for two months."

"It should be sprayed with something," the little old man suggested helpfully.

Again the overweight councilman spoke up. "All that reweaving and all that spraying, and you've still got a flag with forty-eight stars. You're not facing up to the issue as stated by Mr Hackpole."

Three of his peers glared at him, and Mr Cooper said, "I, for one, am opposed to the purchase of a costly flag to satisfy a single taxpayer. It's not in the budget."

A lively discussion ensued.

"We wouldn't have to buy an expensive one."

"Who needs embroidered stars?"

"Yes, but would a cheap flag project the image we want for the city of Pickax?"

"To heck with image!"

"Why not embroider two more stars on the flag we have? I would be glad to undertake it myself if my eyesight —"

"Where do you think you'd put them? On a red stripe? That would look god-awful!" This was Amanda's comment.

"It would not be legal."

"We'd be defacing the flag of the United States."

"Why not get an ordinary printed flag? It doesn't have to be as fancy as this one."

"That solution doesn't eliminate the affront to the donor, rest her soul." This was the elderly councilwoman.

"Then buy a fancy one with gold fringe and send the bill to Hawaii and Alaska. They're the ones with all the money."

There were cheers from the audience.

Mayor Blythe wielded the gavel. "We have a four-horned dilemma here. We can keep the present flag and offend Mr Hackpole. We can replace it and offend the memory of the original donor. We can buy a cheap substitute and sully the city's image. Or we can buy an expensive flag with funds that might better be applied to the new municipal parking lot. I would entertain a motion to table this issue and proceed with further business, assuring Mr Hackpole that his objection will be given due consideration." The flag issue was tabled; the forty-eight stars and thirteen stripes were saluted by all except Mr Hackpole, and the council applied its brainpower to more important matters: barking dogs, the watering of the downtown flowerboxes, and a request from the waterbed store for permission to install a Cuddle Room in which prospective customers might test the product.

At the conclusion of the business meeting the mayor said, "Before we adjourn I would like to introduce a distinguished guest and new resident of Pickax — Mr James Qwilleran."

The benevolent heir to the Klingenschoen fortune — impressively tall and hefty and moustached — rose and bowed graciously. He was greeted by applause and cheers, but no whistles, this being Pickax.

"Mr Mayor, members of the council, ladies and gentlemen," he began, "it is a pleasure to join a community imbued with such sensitive concern, cogent awareness, and vigilant sense of responsibility. I have listened with rapt attention to the flag discussion, and I should like to propose a solution. First I suggest that you preserve the present flag as a memorial to the donor and as a historic artifact, mounting it on the wall under glass. Second, I urge you to accept my gift of a new custom-made, all-wool, silk-lined, floor-standing flag with hand-stitched stripes, embroidered stars, and gold fringe, to be ordered through Amanda's Studio of Interior Design."

The cheers were vociferous, and the demonstration ended with a standing ovation. Qwilleran raised his hand for silence. "You are all aware of the historic Klingenschoen mansion on the Circle. It is my intention that it will eventually be donated to the city of Pickax as a museum." More cheers. "Meanwhile, its priceless treasures are being preserved professionally by our new house manager, who will function as conservator, registrar, and curator of the collection. She is an authority with impeccable credentials, who comes to us from Down

Below. May I present Iris Cobb? Mrs Cobb, will you please stand?"

Mrs Cobb's eyes glistened more brightly than the rhinestones on her glasses as she took her bow. And when the meeting adjourned, Penelope said in slightly crisp tones, "Indeed, Mr Qwilleran, you were a wellspring of surprises this evening."

She drove them home but declined to join them in a celebratory nightcap. "My brother is waiting for me at the office," she explained. "We are pleading a case in court tomorrow, and there are momentous decisions to make before we call it a day."

Mrs Cobb also excused herself. "You'll think I'm silly, Mr Qwilleran, but I want to have a good cry. If only my husband was alive and could hear the applause tonight and see me taking a bow! And your wonderful introduction! It was all so — so thrilling!" She ran upstairs.

Qwilleran went to the library to gaze in panic at the growing pyramid of mail on his desk. Fearing that his gift of a flag would result in even more saccharine letters of commendation, he telephoned the Mooseville postmistress at her home. Her husband answered.

"Hi, Nick. How's everything in Mooseville?"

"Perfect temperature, Qwill, but we need rain. I saw you out biking the other day. Where'd you get that relic?"

"It could use a paint job," Qwilleran admitted, "but it works. I like biking. It gives me time to think. What I don't like is a dog barking at my heels."

"They're not allowed to run loose in this county.

You could make a complaint to the police. That's a violation."

"Well, I always bellow a few choice words, and so far I haven't lost a foot. How's Lori? Is she still working?"

"Not for long," Nick said. "She's put in her resignation."

"She wrote to me about part-time secretarial work."

"Sure thing. I'll put her on."

A vivacious Lori came on the line. "Hello, Qwill. Did you get my letter?"

Immediately Koko was on the desk, nudging the phone and trying to bite the cord. He knew who was on the other end of the line. Qwilleran pushed him away.

"I did indeed, Lori, and there are two bushels of letters here, waiting for you. If Nick wants to pick them up, you can answer them at home."

"Super!"

"You're an expert typist, and your machine is much better than mine."

"Thank you. Nick gave me an electronic for my birthday. I really wanted some little diamond earrings, but he's so practical. An engineer, you know."

"I also want to ask a question, Lori, since you're so knowledgeable about cats." Qwilleran was fighting for possession of the telephone. "Koko likes to sit on the grand staircase, but only on the third stair. How do you explain that behavior?" He gave Koko another shove.

Lori said, "Cats leave their individual scent wherever they go, and they like to return to the same spot. It's like their private territory."

"Hmmm," Qwilleran mused. "Perhaps you're right."

* * *

It was still only ten-thirty, and he was finishing a letter to the Pickax Thespians, declining their invitation to play the role of Teddy in *Arsenic and Old Lace*, when he heard a snatch of music.

From the drawing room came three distinct notes: E, D, C. Koko was playing the piano again. At least, Qwilleran presumed it was Koko at the keyboard, although he had never actually witnessed the cat pressing the keys. No doubt Mrs Cobb would attribute the performance to the resident ghost.

Going to investigate, he found Koko ambling around the drawing room with conspicuous nonchalance. Qwilleran picked him up and plunked him without ceremony on the piano bench. "Now let's hear you play something."

Koko said, "ik ik ik," in a pleasant voice and rolled over to lick his nether parts.

"Don't be modest. Show me what you can do." Qwilleran set the cat back on his four feet and then guided one paw to the keyboard. Twisting like a pretzel, Koko squirmed out of the man's grasp, jumped to the floor, and walked away with stiff-legged hauteur, returning to his perch on the third stair.

Was it coincidence that the notes coming from the piano had been the opening phrase of "Three Blind Mice"? Qwilleran felt the familiar tickle on his upper lip. There was some significance, he felt, to the number three. Three-base hit . . . three-dollar bill . . . three sheets to the wind . . . the three Weird Sisters . . . three-mile limit. Clues eluded him completely.

The next morning Qwilleran was having his third cup of coffee when Amanda Goodwinter arrived unexpectedly, giving the doorbell her three impatient rings.

She barged into the vestibule, wearing an unkempt khaki suit and canvas golf hat, with wisps of hair escaping from underneath the brim. "Came to see if my painter is loafing on the job," she announced.

Qwilleran marveled that Penelope could look so sleek in a suit and Amanda could look so frumpy — the sleeves too long, one shoulder drooping, and the blouse collar half-in and half-out.

"What's that infernal racket?" she demanded.

"Birch Tree is doing some repairs for us," Qwilleran said. "Excuse me a moment. I have something to give you." From a locked drawer in the library desk he brought an ivory elephant. "I think this belongs to you."

"Where the devil did you find this?" She turned the carving over to verify the label.

"Among Daisy Mull's belongings. I was cleaning out the attic."

"It must be six years since this disappeared from the studio," the designer said. "Daisy was working for me then, but it was an election year, and I thought some sneaky Republican made off with it." She handed the carving back to Qwilleran. "Here! It's yours. It's a good one — old — can't import them anymore."

"No! No! It's your property, Amanda."

"Shut up and keep it," she barked at him. "I've already taken a loss on the books. What did you think of the meeting last night?"

"It was refreshing to hear public servants speaking English. No prioritizing. No impacticizing. No decontextualizing."

"Your speech was a corker — all that bosh about vigilant awareness and cogent concern. It gave me a bellyache, but they fell for it."

"By the way, who's Mr Hackpole?" Qwilleran asked.

"He gives *everybody* a bellyache. Always throwing a monkey wrench in the works. Steer clear of Hackpole. He's bad news."

"The overweight councilman seemed to side with him in the flag dispute."

"That's Scott Gippel — scared to death of Hackpole. They're next-door neighbors. Hackpole never pulled a shotgun on anybody *yet*, but he can get gol-durned mad if somebody steps on his grass or complains about his dogs."

"What's his problem?"

"Wife ran off with a beer-truck driver, and he went bonkers. Didn't affect his financial savvy, though. He sells used cars. Sharp operator! . . . Well, let's go and look at the paint job. You ought to keep this back door locked. Bloody tourist season, you know. Town's full of creeps, stoned to the gills. They broke into Dr Hal's office. Took drugs and needles."

As they approached the garage Qwilleran said, "Look at this big wardrobe. I thought it was junk, but Mrs Cobb says it's a Pennsylvania *Schrank* and highly collectible."

Amanda snorted. "Looks like junk to me."

"Well, I'd like your porters to move it into the house when they have time. I'd like to put it just outside the library."

"Arrgh!" she growled. Puffing and grunting, she climbed the stairs to inspect the apartment under renovation. After threatening to fire Steve if he didn't show some signs of life, she had another incredulous look at Daisy's murals and then said to Qwilleran, "Walk me to my car."

As they walked down the driveway under ancient maple trees, Qwilleran remarked about the glorious weather.

"Wait till you've spent a winter here, mister!" Then she added, "Got some advice for you. Watch your step in Pickax. The town likes to gossip. Somebody's always listening. Seems like the whole town's bugged. Wouldn't be surprised if they bugged the flowerboxes on Main Street. I don't trust our mayor either. Nice fella, but I don't trust him as far as I can spit. So keep your eyes and ears open, and don't say anything you don't want repeated."

"At the coffee shop, you mean?"

"Or at the country club. Or on the church steps."

Amanda climbed into the driver's seat with some awkward maneuvering of knees, elbows, and hips. She gunned the motor and her car shot down the driveway, stopped short with squealing tires, and backed up. "And watch out for my cousins! Don't be fooled by the phony Goodwinter charm."

She took off again, barreling recklessly into the traffic flow around the Circle.

Qwilleran was baffled. Pickax was full of Goodwinters, and they were all cousins. There was nothing phony about Melinda. He liked her humor — sometimes cynical, usually irreverent. She had just returned from Paris, and he had made a date with her, anticipating a relaxing evening of conversation, if not more. Melinda had been aggressively seductive from the beginning.

"Is that good or bad?" he said aloud when he returned to the house to feed the cats. "What would you guys like for breakfast? Veal Oscar? *Coq au vin?* Shrimp deJonghe?" He diced some of Mrs Cobb's pot roast and arranged it on a Royal Worcester plate with pan juices, a little grated carrot, and a sprinkling of hard-cooked egg yolks. "*Voilà,*" he said.

Both cats attacked the meal with gusto, carefully avoiding the grated carrot.

His next visitor was Tiffany Trotter, the same wholesome, robust country girl who had interviewed for the job of housekeeper. This time they talked in the library to avoid the noise of Birch's hammering and sawing and radio; he was now building shelves for Mrs Cobb's reference books.

In the library Tiffany swiveled her eyes over the book-filled shelves and sculptured plaster ceiling. "This is a pretty room," she said.

"You wanted to speak to me about Daisy," Qwilleran reminded her.

"She used to work here."

"I'm aware of that. Are you a friend of Daisy's?"

"We were very good friends, and —" She shrugged for want of the right words. "I thought it was kinda funny when she left town without telling me — didn't even write." She searched Qwilleran's face for his reaction.

"Did you make inquiries at that time?"

"I asked the old lady she worked for, and she said Daisy moved to Florida. She acted as if she was mad about something."

"That was five years ago. How long had you been friends?"

"Since ninth grade. The Dimsdale kids were bused to Pickax, and the other kids made fun of Daisy because she was a Mull. I kinda liked her. She was different. She could draw."

"Did she have boyfriends?"

"Not till she left school. She didn't finish. She didn't like school."

"Do you know who her friends were?"

"Just guys."

"She was pregnant when she left. Did you know that?"

"Mmmm . . . yes."

"Did she say anything about getting an abortion?"

"Oh, no!" Tiffany was emphatic for the first time during the interview. "She wanted the baby. She wanted to get married, but I don't think the guy wanted to."

"Who was the father?"

"Mmmm . . . I dunno."

"What did Daisy's mother think about all of this?"

Tiffany shrugged. "I dunno. She never talked about her mother. They didn't get along."

"Mrs Mull died a few days ago. Did you know?"

"Somebody told me."

It was one of those moments when Qwilleran would have relished a smoke. Puffing a Scottish blend in his old quarterbend bulldog would have sharpened his mental processes, would have given him pauses in which to organize his questions. But Melinda had urged him to give up his comfortable old pipe.

He asked the girl if she would like a beer, thinking it would help her relax; she was sitting on the edge of the blood-red leather sofa.

"I guess not," she said. "I hafta go and do the milking."

"Do you think something bad might have happened to your friend?"

Tiffany moistened her lips. "I dunno. I just thought it was funny when she went away and didn't tell me. Nobody else cared, so that's why I came."

As Qwilleran accompanied her to the front door, Birch was shifting his tools and radio to another place of operation. "Whatcha doin' here, sweetheart?" he called out in his hearty voice. "Lookin' for a job? Whatsa matter with that big bozo you married? I thought you'd be knocked up by now. Baa-a-a-a!"

Tiffany gave the man a sideways glance and a timid smile, and Qwilleran said to him, "Skip the social pleasantries, Birch. Just tell us when we're going to get a lock on the back door."

"Came in yesterday — airmail from Down Below," Birch said. "You'll have it tomorrow. No lie."

Qwilleran watched Tiffany leave. She crossed the little park and drove away in a pickup that had been parked on the far side of the Circle. Why hadn't she parked in the driveway? There was ample space. Her wordless reaction to Birch's remark had been equally puzzling.

"Dammit!" Qwilleran said aloud. He should have asked her why she came to see him. Who told her he was interested?

There's something going on here that I don't know about, he thought, and she knows something she's not telling. That's the way it is in a small town. It's all very friendly and open on the surface, but underneath it's a network of intrigue and secrecy.

CHAPTER NINE

Qwilleran and Melinda dined at the Old Stone Mill, a former gristmill converted into a restaurant by dedicated preservationists who cared more about historic landmarks than about the seasoning of the soup. Yet, the atmosphere was inviting and conducive to intimate conversation. He ordered champagne, to celebrate her return, and something innocuous for himself.

"How was Paris?" he asked.

"Full of Americans. The next conference will be in Australia. You should go with me, lover."

Too expensive, he thought. Then he realized the words no longer belonged in his vocabulary. He was finding it difficult to adjust to his new financial status.

"I don't like traveling alone," Melinda was saying. "I don't even like living alone." Her green eyes flickered invitingly.

"Watch those fluttering eyelashes," Qwilleran said. "We haven't even had the soup yet."

"Any excitement while I was away?"

In graphic detail he described the Great Flag Controversy. "I'm curious about Blythe," he said. "He's articulate and conducts a meeting exceptionally well. Who is he? What's his background?"

"He's an investment counselor. His mother was a

Goodwinter. He was principal of the high school until the scandal a few years ago."

"What happened?" As a journalist Qwilleran felt professionally privileged to pry.

"He was involved with some girl students, but he got off with a slap on the wrist and an invitation to resign. Anyone else would have left town in disgrace, but he's got the Goodwinter guts. He ran for mayor and won by a landslide."

At Melinda's urging they ordered ravioli. "It's the specialty of the house. They buy it frozen, and it's the only thing on the menu that the cook can't ruin."

"This town really needs a good restaurant."

"The Lanspeaks are opening one — haven't you heard? They travel a lot and appreciate good food, so it should be an oasis in a desert of French fries and ketchup . . . How's everything at the Pickax Palace?"

"Mrs Cobb finally arrived. And I've ordered a suede sofa for my studio. And at last we have a lock on the back door. Birch Tree comes almost every day to do the repairs and play his obscene radio. Today he went fishing, and it was so quiet the cats walked around on tiptoe."

"Is Koko still throwing your female guests out of the house at eleven p.m.?"

"That's his bedtime," Qwilleran explained apologetically. "Not only can that cat tell time, but I believe he can count. He sits on the *third stair* of the staircase all the time."

"Third from the top or third from the bottom? If he's counting from the top, it's more likely he's sitting on the eighteenth stair." The green eyes were impudent.

Then Qwilleran told her about the three-foot candelabra in the silver vault. "If I decide to give a dinner party, will you consent to be my hostess?"

"Or anything else, lover," she said with a green-eyed wink.

"My editor from the *Fluxion* is flying up to spend a few days, and I thought I might invite Penelope and Alexander and a few others from Pickax and Mooseville. Mrs Cobb has offered to cook."

"Is she good?"

"Well, she does the world's best pot roast and coconut cake and macaroni-and-cheese."

"Darling, you can't serve macaroni-and-cheese with three-foot silver candelabra on the table. You should have something elegant: six courses, starting with *escargots* . . . a butler serving cocktails in the solarium . . . two footmen to serve in the dining room . . . a string trio going crazy behind the potted palms."

"You're not serious, I hope," Qwilleran said warily.

"Of course I'm serious. There's no time to send out engraved invitations, so you'll have to telephone everyone, although it's not good form for a formal dinner."

"Who'll know the difference?"

"*Penelope* will know," Melinda said with a mocking grin. "Penelope still eats ice cream with a fork. Socially she's a throwback to the Edwardian era. My great-grandmother owned sixteen etiquette books. In those days people didn't worry about losing weight or getting in touch with their feelings; they wanted to know if they should eat mashed potatoes with a knife."

She declined dessert and finished the bottle of champagne, but Qwilleran ordered French-fried ice cream, a cannonball of pastry reposing in a puddle of chocolate sauce. No matter how he attacked the impenetrable crust, the ball merely rotated in the slippery sauce and threatened to bounce to the floor.

With each sip of champagne Melinda was becoming more elated about the party. "To impress your editor we ought to serve foods indigenous to this area, starting with terrine of pheasant and jellied watercress consommé. There's a secret cove on the Ittibittiwassee — accessible only by canoe — where one can find watercress. Do you canoe?"

"Only in reverse," Qwilleran said.

"How about Chinook salmon croquettes for the fish course?" She took another sip of champagne. "The entrée could be lamb *bûcheronne* with tiny Moose County potatoes and mushrooms. It's too dry to find morels." Another sip. "Then a salad of homegrown asparagus vinaigrette. How does that sound?"

"Don't forget dessert. Preferably not French-fried ice cream."

"How about a wild raspberry trifle? We'll need two or three wines, but I can steal those from Dad's wine cellar."

"I hope butlers and footmen are indigenous to Moose County," Qwilleran said.

"That poses a problem," Melinda admitted, "but . . . we might get actors from the Pickax Thespians. Larry Lanspeak played the title role in *Jeeves*, and he'd make a perfect butler."

"You don't mean the owner of the department store, do you?"

"Sure! He'd love it! The Fitch twins are home from Yale, and they could wear their costumes from *The Student Prince* and play the footmen. We'd have a rehearsal, of course, and they'd play their roles with a straight face . . . Penelope will have a fit!"

Qwilleran believed not a word of it, but he was enjoying Melinda's champagne fantasy. "Where will we get a string trio?"

She closed her eyes in thought. "Dad talks about three musicians who used to play Strauss waltzes behind the potted palms at the Pickax Hotel before World War Two."

"By now they're all dead, Melinda."

"Not necessarily. People live a long time in Moose County."

As they left the restaurant he said, "Your scenario has been a lot of fun. I only wish we could swing it."

"Of course we can swing it!" she said indignantly. "I have my mother's recipes, and I'll work out the details with Mrs Cobb. All you have to do is pay the bills."

They went to Melinda's condo to look at her great-grandmother's etiquette books, and Qwilleran arrived home at a late hour, humming a tune from *The Student Prince*. As he turned the key in the new back-door lock, he could hear Koko scolding severely.

"You mind your own business," Qwilleran told him. "Go and fraternize with Yum Yum."

Before retiring he made his nightly house check, turning on lights in all the rooms, inspecting windows and

French doors, taking a hasty inventory of French bronzes, Chinese porcelains, Venetian glass, and Georgian silver. Everything was in order except in the kitchen, where the step stool was situated unaccountably in the center of the room.

When Qwilleran reported this manifestation to Mrs Cobb the next morning, she said, "I told you something spooky was happening. Now you'll believe me! What's more, I heard someone fooling around with the piano keys last night after the lights were out."

Qwilleran was scheduled to address a luncheon meeting of the Pickax Boosters Club at noon and then pick up Arch Riker at the airport. But first he telephoned his dinner invitations. Everyone accepted with pleasure, despite the short notice.

Penelope said, "My brother returns from Washington this evening. We shall be delighted to attend. Black tie?"

"Optional," Qwilleran said. "Melinda wants you to know she's wearing a long dress."

"Splendid!"

When he called Amanda she was exultant. "Nobody's invited me to cocktails and dinner in a coon's age! I'll drag my long dress out of the cedar closet."

To Junior Goodwinter he said, "Don't bring your notebook. You're invited as a guest, not a reporter. And see if you can borrow a tie somewhere."

Before going to his luncheon meeting Qwilleran himself bought a new tie at Scottie's Men's Shop, although he thought the price exorbitant.

There were no feed caps at the Boosters luncheon.

All the influential men of the community gathered in a private room — at the Old Stone Mill for frozen ravioli à la microwave. Among those he recognized were Mayor Blythe, Dr Halifax Goodwinter, Chief Brodie, and the dour Mr Cooper. Since President Goodwinter was still in Washington and Vice-President Lanspeak had trans-Pacific jet lag, Nigel Fitch introduced the guest speaker with flowery accolades.

"Gentlemen," Qwilleran began, "it was my previous understanding that Down Below referred to a geographic location. Now I realize it's something else. While we enjoy perfect temperatures in Moose County, it's hot as hell Down Below." There was hearty applause from the Boosters.

"Fine weather," he went on, "is not the only reason I'm happy to be here. Since arriving I have not once been mugged, or asphyxiated by carbon monoxide, or knocked down by a truck." (More applause.) "On the debit side, I have had to give up whistling." (Laughter from all except Cooper.)

"Having worked all my life, I feel the need to engage in some worthwhile enterprise in this area. I have considered opening an exercise studio next door to Otto's Tasty Eats." (Chuckles.) "Or I might acquire the mosquito-repellant franchise for Mooseville." (Loud laughter.) "Or start a driver's training school." (Roars of laughter.)

He then went on to explain the aims of the Klingenschoen Foundation, and as he bowed to the final applause Mayor Blythe presented him with a genuine pickax in good working order.

After adjournment the hardware merchant introduced himself. "I understand you're starting to lock your back door, Mr Qwilleran. Not a bad idea, the way things are going. I special-ordered your lock from Down Below. Beautiful mechanism! Top of the line!"

Then the police chief led Qwilleran aside. "You were talking to me about that girl who disappeared five years ago. You said she was last seen on July seventh."

"That's the last day she worked, according to our employment records."

"There was something about that date that rang a bell," Brodie said. "I was a sheriff's deputy then. There was a big cave-in at one of the mines on the night of July seventh. We had it roped off, I remember, until they could put up a fence. Kept a deputy there twenty-four hours a day. Just thought I'd mention it."

A smooth-looking sandy-haired man introduced himself as Sam Gafner, a real estate broker. Qwilleran knew he was a salesman before he opened his mouth. "Interested in a business opportunity, Mr Q? I happen to know this restaurant is going on the block very soon. Beautiful piece of property; all it needs is some good food management."

With applause and compliments elevating his mood, Qwilleran drove to the airport to meet Arch Riker.

The editor stepped off the plane and looked around in dismay. "Is this the airport? Is that the terminal? I thought we'd made an emergency landing on a softball field and the shack with a wind sock was the dugout."

Qwilleran grabbed his hand. "Good to see you, Arch. How was the flight?"

"Like flying with the Wright brothers."

Qwilleran steered him to the Klingenschoen limousine. "I hope you brought your dinner jacket, Arch."

With Riker's luggage stowed in the trunk, the sleek black vehicle purred down the long stretch of Airport Road.

"Ten miles of straight road without a curve, hill, crossroad, or habitation," Qwilleran boasted. "Nothing to worry about except deer, elk, raccoons, skunks, and the state police. There's a lot of wild game around here. Everybody goes hunting, pronounced '*huntn*.' Everybody has a *huntn* rifle and *huntn* dogs . . . Where you see warning signs, those are abandoned mines."

"Spooky-looking places," Riker said. "I'll bet the kids use the old shaft houses for their wild parties. How do you like living in the wilderness?"

Qwilleran thought, Wait till he sees the butler and the string trio. "Fine! I like it fine! And the cats are going crazy, chasing around the big rooms. Koko can fly up twenty-one stairs in two leaps."

"Has he learned any new tricks?"

"Arch, that crazy animal has started playing post office. When the mail comes, he sorts it out and brings me the letters he considers important."

"Nobody else would believe that, but I do."

"It's a fact. He seems to detect certain scents. He's brought me letters from persons he knows, households that have cats, and places where he used to live."

"I hear Mrs Cobb is working for you," Riker said, verging on a touchy subject.

"We'll talk about that when we get home and settle

down with a drink," Qwilleran said. "How's everything at the *Flux*?"

"I'm just serving time until I can collect my pension."

"Wait till you see the *Pickax Picayune*! You need a magnifying glass to read the headlines. They cover all the ice cream socials and chicken dinners."

"What do you do for news?"

"Fortunately the state edition of the *Flux* is distributed up here, and that keeps us in touch with reality — wars, disasters, assassinations, riots, mass murders, all the worthwhile news. WPKX keeps us informed of car accidents, hunting mishaps, and barn fires." He turned on the radio. "We've just missed the six o'clock news, I'm afraid."

The announcer was saying, ". . . when she fell from a tractor on a farm owned by her father, Terence Kilcally, forty-eight. The tractor then entered a ditch and overturned. Sheriff deputies told WPKX that the tractor continued to travel until it entered a ditch and rolled over . . . Present temperature in Pickax, a pleasant seventy-five degrees."

"Pickax doesn't need air-conditioning," Qwilleran said as he pointed out the important houses on Goodwinter Boulevard. "These stone buildings stay cool all summer. They have walls two feet thick."

And then they reached the K mansion. Riker, jaded after twenty-odd years of editing sensational news, was nonetheless stunned by its grandeur. "Nobody lives like this, Qwill! Least of all you! It's a little Versailles! It's the Buckingham Palace of the north woods!"

"Quit writing headlines, Arch, and tell me what you want to drink."

"I'm back on martinis, but I'll mix my own. Since you've been on the wagon you've lost your touch."

Qwilleran poured white grape juice for himself and a thimbleful for Koko.

"He remembers me," said Riker as the cat rubbed against his ankles.

"He knows you have cats at home. How's old Punky? How's old Mibs?"

"Let's go and sit down," Riker said with sudden weariness. They took their drinks to the solarium. "Well, it's like this," he said in a tremulous voice. "We had them put to sleep. It was a rough decision to make, but Rosie didn't want them, and the house was up for sale, and I moved to a hotel. Nobody wants to adopt old animals, so . . . I asked the vet to put them away. They were beautiful longhairs, and he didn't want to do it, but . . . I had no choice."

Both men were silent as Koko and Yum Yum sauntered into the room, nestled together on a cushioned wicker chair, and started licking each other.

"Where's Mrs Cobb?" Riker asked finally.

"She went to a meeting of the Historical Society. I was surprised to hear she'd sold her antique shop."

"*You* were surprised? How do you think I felt? Rosie got a little inheritance, and next thing I knew, she bought out the Cobb business and announced she was going to live over the store — on Zwinger Street! That crummy neighborhood!"

"What happened to Rosie, Arch? I knew she went back to school after the kids left home."

"She took a few college courses and got in with a young crowd — got some new ideas, I guess. Young people have always liked Rosie; she's full of life. But there's something sad about mature people who suddenly try to return to their youth — especially a middle-aged woman with a young lover."

Qwilleran combed his moustache with his knuckles. "What about middle-aged men with young partners?"

Riker thought about it. "That's different, somehow."

Qwilleran suggested the Old Stone Mill for dinner. "Don't expect great food, but the atmosphere's pleasant, and we can have a little privacy."

They sat at a window table overlooking the great mill wheel, which still turned and creaked without benefit of a millstream. It was powered electrically, with taped sound effects giving the impression of rushing water.

Riker relaxed. "Bucolic tranquillity! Makes one wonder why we live in cities. Don't you miss the criminal activity Down Below? You always enjoyed a good murder."

Qwilleran lowered his voice. "To tell the truth, Arch, there's a situation here that's got me wondering. A girl disappeared from the K mansion five years ago, and I've been getting the old familiar vibrations."

He told Riker about the murals, the four notes played on the antique piano, and Koko's discovery of Daisy's luggage in the attic. "The real tip-off was a postal card supposed to be from Daisy but not in her handwriting.

I found out the girl was pregnant and the guy wouldn't marry her."

"Nowadays it doesn't matter a whole lot, does it? My daughter wants a child but no husband. We're an endangered species."

"This case was different, Arch. Here was a girl from the *wrong side* of the wrong side of the tracks, and marriage would be a chance to change her name. Just as I was about to visit her mother and ask a few questions, the woman died of accidental substance abuse — or so the coroner decided."

"You always get mixed up in these things," Riker said, "and I don't know why. Who played the piano? Don't tell me it was the cat!"

"Who knows? I also heard the opening notes of 'Three Blind Mice'. And if it wasn't Koko, we've got an apparition on the premises. Take your pick."

They returned to the house shortly after dark. Flickering blue lights in an upstairs window indicated that Mrs Cobb had retired to watch television.

"Nightcap?" Qwilleran suggested to his guest.

At that moment they both heard four notes played on the piano in the drawing room: E, E, E, C — loud and clear.

Riker was startled. "What was that?"

"Beethoven's Fifth," Qwilleran said. "Now will you believe me?"

They sat at the kitchen table and listened to the eleven o'clock news on WPKX:

"The annexation battle between city and county became a slugging match at a public hearing this evening when a township supervisor was assaulted by an angry resident. Clem Wharton declined to press charges against his assailant, Herb Hackpole.

"The school board tonight voted unanimously in favor of quality education. Board president Ninikoff told WPKX, 'We've put ourselves on the line in favor of quality education.'

"It was earlier reported that a Pickax Township woman was killed in a fall from a tractor on her father's farm. According to the coroner's report, Tiffany Trotter, twenty-two, was killed by a gunshot wound. Police are investigating."

CHAPTER TEN

Qwilleran passed a sleepless night. He was concerned about his friend's marital breakup. He was apprehensive about hosting an ambitious dinner party. And he felt uneasy about the murder of Tiffany Trotter.

He had told Riker about her interest in Daisy, adding, "If there's a connection between her visit here and her murder, it means I'm on a hot scent."

"It also means you could be on the hit list yourself," the editor had said. "Better cool it, Qwill."

At an early hour the telephone rang, and Amanda Goodwinter plunged into the conversation with her usual brashness. "Got a problem. Got to find another painter to finish your apartment. Not easy to do these days. Nobody wants to work."

"What happened?" Qwilleran asked in the early-morning stupor that followed an unsatisfactory sleep.

"Didn't you hear the news? Tiffany Trotter was shot."

He was slow in putting two and two together. "Uh . . . yes . . . I heard it on the radio."

"That's Steve's wife," Amanda shouted impatiently. "Steve, my painter! He won't be back on the job for a while."

"I didn't get the connection," Qwilleran said. "That's a terrible thing. We don't expect that in Moose County, do we?"

"Tourists! That's what's wrong," the designer grumbled. "Coming up here in their fancy painted vans. They're all *stoned*, I tell you!"

"Is that what the police think? I haven't heard any details."

"Francesca says — that's my assistant; her father is chief of police — Francesca says they think it was a sniper — some psycho who just happened to be driving past the farm with a high-powered rifle. These kooks from Down Below have been known to shoot crows, but this is outrageous!"

"Is Brodie handling the investigation?"

"It's the sheriff's turf but the Pickax police cooperate."

As Amanda rambled on, conjectures raced through Qwilleran's mind: Not necessarily a tourist; everyone in the county has a hunting rifle . . . The husband is always the first suspect. There could be a dozen different reasons why an enemy or a neighbor or even a relative might pull the trigger . . . Who are these Trotters? Are they involved in anything shady?

Amanda was saying, "So I'm trying to get Steve's cousin to finish the job."

"No hurry. It can wait till Steve comes back."

"Shucks, I want the job finished so I can get my money! Carpet's waiting to be laid. The blinds are ready . . . Say, I'm all excited about your party. Hope you've got some good bourbon."

Qwilleran said, "I think you'll like our visitor from

Down Below. Arch Riker is an editor from the *Daily Fluxion*."

"I'll be on my good behavior, unless my cousins provoke me, and then *look out*!"

"May we pick you up? I'll send Arch over with the limousine."

"Hot damn!" said Amanda.

Qwilleran and Riker took a walk downtown during the morning hours, to view the bizarre street scene — eight centuries of Old World architecture condensed into two commercial blocks. The department store posed as a Byzantine palace. The gas station looked like Stonehenge.

At the *Picayune* office they introduced themselves to Junior's father, owner and publisher of the newspaper. Senior Goodwinter was a mild-mannered man, wearing a leather apron and a square paper cap made of folded newsprint.

"Is it true you hand-set most of the type yourself?" Qwilleran asked.

"Been doing it since I was eight. Had to stand on a stool to reach the typecases," Senior said proudly. "It's the best part of the business."

Riker said, "The *Picayune* is the only paper I know that has successfully resisted twentieth-century technology and new trends in journalism."

"Thank you," said the publisher. "It hasn't changed in any way since it was founded by my great-grandfather."

From there the two men walked to the office of Goodwinter & Goodwinter. Qwilleran apologized to

Penelope for dropping in without an appointment. "I simply wanted to introduce Mr Riker and request some information."

"Come into the conference room," she said graciously, but her automatic smiles and dimples faded when he put his question:

"Do you know anything about the Trotter girl who was murdered?"

"What do you mean?" she asked sharply.

"Do you have any inside information about the young woman, her family, her activities? Any theories about the murder? Was it a random killing or is there some local intrigue, some shady connection?"

"I'm afraid you've come to the wrong place, Mr Qwilleran. This is a law firm — not a detective agency or a social services office." There was a sarcastic edge to her voice. "May I inquire why you ask these peculiar questions?"

"Sorry. I should have explained," Qwilleran said. "My first impulse, on hearing about the murder, was to establish a scholarship for farm youth as a memorial to Tiffany Trotter. I'm assuming she was an innocent victim. If there is anything unsavory about her character or connections, my idea would not be exactly appropriate."

The attorney relaxed. "I see what you mean, but I'm unable to give you an immediate answer. My brother and I will take it under advisement. We are both looking forward to your dinner tomorrow evening."

Walking away from the Goodwinter office Qwilleran said to Riker, "I've never seen her quite so edgy. She's working too hard. Her brother spends half his time in Washington — doing God-knows-what — and she has to handle the practice single-handed."

Exactly at noon the siren on the roof of the City Hall blasted its hair-raising wail. At that signal everything in Pickax closed for an hour, allowing workers to go home to lunch. No taxes or traffic tickets were paid; no automobiles or candy bars were sold; no prescriptions or teeth were filled. Only emergency services and one small downtown restaurant continued to operate.

Qwilleran and Riker went into the luncheonette for a sandwich and listened to the buzz of voices. There was only one topic of conversation:

"They weren't married more than a year. She made her own wedding dress."

"Tiff made more kills last year than anybody in the volleyball league."

"My brother was Steve's best man. All the fellas wore white tailcoats and white top hats. Really cool!"

When the two men returned home there was an unfamiliar truck parked near the garage, its body mounted high over the chassis.

"What's that ugly thing doing there?" Riker asked.

"Don't knock it," Qwilleran said. "A terrain vehicle up here has the *éclat* of a private jet Down Below. Farmers and sportsmen love 'em. I'll go and see whose it is."

In the loft above the garage he found a substitute painter putting the finish coat on the doorframes. "Are you Steve's cousin?"

"Yeah, I'm fillin' in till he gets back."

"I feel very bad about Tiffany."

"Yeah, it's tough. And you wanna know what? The police took Steve in for questioning! Ain't that a kick in the head?"

"It's only routine," Qwilleran assured him. "The police think the sniper was a tourist."

The painter looked wise and said in a lowered voice, "I could tell 'em a few things, but I know when to keep my mouth shut."

Typical small-town reaction, Qwilleran thought. Everyone knows the answers, or thinks he does, or pretends to. But no one talks.

Riker had found a hammock in the backyard and was reading the *Picayune.* Mrs Cobb was in the kitchen, pounding boned pheasant for the terrine.

"The police were here!" she announced. "They wanted to know if Steve was on the job yesterday afternoon, and I was able to give him an alibi. He was having a beer with me at the time of the shooting. He's a nice young man. I feel very sorry for him."

"It's abnormally quiet. Where's Birch?"

"Gone fishing. He's catching the salmon for the croquettes."

"Is everything progressing to your satisfaction?"

"Everything's getting done, but Koko's been acting funny, scratching the broom closet door and jumping up to reach the handle."

"I put that musty suitcase in the closet, and he can smell it. He doesn't miss a thing. It's time I got rid of all that junk."

Koko heard his name and came running, saying, "ik ik ik," in a businesslike tone.

"Okay, okay, I'm throwing the smelly things out." Qwilleran carried the large carton of Daisy's winter clothing to the trash bin in the garage and then returned for the suitcase. He was halfway to the back door when he heard an emphatic yowl. It was not the kind of cat-talk that meant "Time for dinner" or "Here comes the mail" or "Where's Yum Yum?" It was a vehement directive.

Qwilleran stopped. Why, he asked himself, had Koko suddenly resumed interest in the suitcase? Not the carton, just the suitcase. Without further hesitation he turned around and carried the piece of luggage to the library. Koko followed in great excitement.

Once again Qwilleran inspected the contents of the suitcase, examining each pathetic item, hoping to find a clue or start a train of thought. He emptied the case right down to the sleazy torn lining.

"Yow!" said Koko, who was supervising the process.

Torn lining! A twinge on Qwilleran's upper lip was telling him something. Speculatively he passed a hand over the bottom of the case. There was the outline of something flat and rectangular beneath the cheap, shiny, stained cloth. When he reached into the rip it tore further and exposed an envelope — a blank white envelope. Inside it was a wad of currency — new bills — hundred-dollar bills — ten of them.

"Yow!" said Koko.

Where, Qwilleran wondered, did she get this much money? Did she steal it? Was it a payoff? A bribe to leave town? The wherewithal for an abortion?

Daisy might not have realized the value of the ivory elephant. She might have forgotten the gold bracelet in her hurry to get away. But if she happened to have a thousand in cash, she would hardly leave town without it . . . that is, if she *had* left town.

After the dinner party, Qwilleran promised himself, he would have another chat with the police chief.

CHAPTER ELEVEN

On the day of the party the house was in turmoil, and the Siamese were banished to the basement — until their indignant protests became more annoying than their actual presence underfoot.

Mrs Cobb was rolling croquettes and slivering lamb with garlic. Mrs Fulgrove was ironing table linens, polishing silver, and writing place cards and gentlemen's envelopes in her flawless penmanship, flattered beyond words when asked to do so. The florist delivered a truckload of flowers. The end sections of the long dinner table had been removed in order to seat ten comfortably, and Melinda was using a yardstick to measure the correct distance between dinner plates.

All this frenzied activity made Qwilleran nervous. He had never hosted a formal dinner; all his entertaining had been done in restaurants and clubs. So, when Riker borrowed the car and went sightseeing, Qwilleran set out for a tranquilizing bike ride.

Having completed the loop that constituted his daily ten-mile workout, he was just within the city limits when a menacing dog with a full set of repulsive teeth bounded from a backyard and charged the bicycle, barking and nipping at his heels. Qwilleran bellowed and swerved to the left and heard a screeching of tires as a motorist behind him jammed on the brakes.

Someone called to the dog, and the animal ran back into the yard, where two others were barking and straining at their chains.

In spluttering fury Qwilleran approached the driver of the car. "That dog — did you see him come at me?"

The woman at the wheel said, "I'm all shook up. I thought sure I was going to hit you. It was terrible! It shouldn't be allowed."

"Allowed! It's not allowed! It's prohibited by law. I'm going to make a formal complaint. May I have your name as a witness?"

She shrank away from him. "I'd really like to help, but . . . my husband wouldn't want me to get involved. I'm terribly sorry."

Qwilleran said no more but biked directly to the police station, where he found Chief Brodie on the desk, growling about a complaint of his own. "Too much paperwork! They invent computers to make life easier, and everything gets complicated. What can I do for you, Mr Q?"

Qwilleran related his experience with the unchained dog, giving the name of the street and the number of the house. "That dog might be rabid," he said, "and I might have been killed."

Brodie made a helpless gesture. "Hackpole again! It's a problem. He's had a lot of warnings. There's nothing more we can do unless you want to go to the magistrate and sign a complaint. Nobody else will stick his neck out."

"Who is Hackpole, anyway? Was he ever a New York cabdriver?"

"He was born here, but he worked in the East for a long time — Newark, I think. Came back a few years ago. Runs a used-car lot and a garage."

"Will it do any good if I sign a complaint?"

"The sheriff will deliver a summons, and there'll be a show-cause hearing in two or three weeks."

"I'll do it!" Qwilleran said. "And tell the sheriff to get an antirabies shot and wear dogproof pants."

When he returned home from his bike ride he was less tranquil than before, but the magnificence of the interior calmed his tensions.

In the dining room, crystal and silver glittered on white damask, and two towering candelabra flanked a Victorian epergne, its branches filled with flowers, fruit, nuts, and mints.

By seven o'clock Melinda had changed into a chiffon dinner dress in a green that enhanced her eyes. Qwilleran, wearing the better of his two suits and his new tie, looked almost well dressed; his hair and moustache were trimmed, and two weeks of biking had given him a tan as well as an improved waistline.

Riker had been dispatched to pick up Amanda. As for the Siamese, it was decided that they be allowed to join the company. Otherwise their nonstop wailing would drown out the efforts of the three elderly men who were tuning their stringed instruments in the foyer.

Playing the role of butler, the genial owner of the department store was rehearsing with starched dignity and a stony countenance. As the footmen, the banker's sons were practicing obsequious anonymity — not easy for Yale undergraduates, Melinda remarked. The Fitch twins would be stationed at the front door to admit guests and conduct them to the solarium, where Lanspeak would announce them and serve cocktails. Later, in the dining room, the footmen would serve from the left and remove plates from the right, while the butler poured wine with a deft twist of the wrist.

"Remember," Melinda told them. "No eye contact."

How did I get mixed up in this? Qwilleran wondered.

First guest to ring the doorbell was the fresh-faced young managing editor of the *Picayune*, looking like a high school student on graduation day. Roger and his wife and mother-in-law arrived in high spirits, Sharon in an Indian sari and Mildred in something she had woven herself, with much fringe. Equally merry were Arch Riker and his blind date, leading Qwilleran to assume they had stopped at a bar. Amanda's floral print dress had the aroma of a cedar closet and look of a thrift shop.

Finally, making their quiet but grand entrance, were Penelope and her brother, Alexander — a tall impressive pair with the lean, high-browed Goodwinter features and an elegant presence. Alexander looked cool and important in a white silk suit, and his sister was cool and chic in a simple white dinner dress. She moved in a cloud of perfume, an arresting fragrance that seemed to take everyone by surprise.

"The Duke and Duchess have arrived," Amanda whispered to Riker. "Mind your manners or it's *off with your head*!"

Qwilleran made the introductions, and Alexander said to Riker in his courtroom voice, "We trust you will find our peaceful little community as enjoyable as we find your — ah — stimulating newspaper."

"I'm certainly enjoying your — ah — perfect weather," said the editor.

Qwilleran inquired about the weather in Washington.

"Unbearably hot," said the attorney with a wry smile, "but one tries to suffer with grace. While I have the ear of — ah — influential persons, I do what I can for our farmers, the forgotten heroes of this great northern county of ours."

The French doors of the solarium were open, admitting early-evening zephyrs that dissipated somewhat the impact of Penelope's perfume. Drifting in from the trio in the foyer were Cole Porter melodies that created the right touch of gaiety and sophistication.

When the butler approached with a silver tray of potables, the Goodwinters recognized the local retailing tycoon and exchanged incredulous glances, but they maintained their poise.

"Champagne, madame," Lanspeak intoned, "and Catawba grape juice."

Penelope hesitated, looked briefly at her brother, and chose the nonalcoholic beverage.

Qwilleran said, "There are mixed drinks if you prefer."

"I consider this an occasion for champagne," Alexander said, taking a glass with a flourish. "History is made tonight. To our knowledge this is the first festive dinner ever to take place at the Klingenschoen mansion."

"The Klingenschoens were never active in the social life of Pickax," his sister said with elevated eyebrows.

The guests circulated, remarked about the size of the rubber plants, admired the Siamese, and made smalltalk.

"Hello, Koko," Roger said bravely, but the cat ignored him. Both Koko and Yum Yum were intent upon circling Penelope, sniffing ardently and occasionally sneezing a delicate whispered *chfff*.

The guest of honor was teasing Sharon about the primitive airport.

"Don't laugh, Mr Riker. My grandmother arrived here in a covered wagon, and that was only seventy-five years ago. Our farms didn't have electricity until 1937."

To Junior, Riker said, "You must be the world's youngest managing editor."

"I'm starting at the top and working my way down," Junior said. "My ambition is to be a copyboy for the *Daily Fluxion*."

"Copy *facilitator*," the editor corrected him.

At a signal from the hostess the butler carried a silver tray of small envelopes to the gentlemen, containing the names of the ladies they were to take into the dining room. "Dinner is served," he announced. The musicians switched to Viennese waltzes, and the guests went in to dinner two by two. No one noticed Koko and Yum Yum bringing up the rear, with tails proudly erect.

Penelope, escorted by Qwilleran, whispered, "Forgive me if I sounded curt yesterday. I had received bad news, although that is no excuse. My brother sees no reason why your memorial to Tiffany Trotter should be inappropriate."

The great doors of the dining room had been rolled back, and the company gasped at the sight. Sixteen wax candles were burning in the silver candelabra, and twenty-four electric candles were aglow in the staghorn chandeliers, all of this against a rich background of linenfold paneling and drawn velvet draperies. There were comments on the magnificent centerpiece. Then the guests savored the terrine of pheasant, and Qwilleran noticed — from the corner of his eye — two dark brown tails disappearing under the white damask.

Seated at the head of the table, he had Penelope on his right and Amanda on his left. At one point he described the incident caused by Hackpole's dog, also his decision to make a formal complaint.

Amanda said, "It's about time somebody blew the whistle on that lamebrain. If our mayor wasn't such an ass, he wouldn't let Hackpole get away with it."

Penelope promptly launched a more genteel topic. "Everyone is tremendously pleased to hear, Mr Qwilleran, that you might present this house to the city as a museum."

"The city won't appreciate it," Amanda retorted. "They'll find it costs a few bucks to heat the place and pay the light bill, and they'll rezone the Circle and sell it for a rooming house."

It seemed to Qwilleran that the conversation at the other end of the table was progressing with more finesse. While he labored to get Roger and Junior talking, he could hear Riker telling newspaper stories, Alexander extolling the social life in Washington, Melinda describing her week in Paris, and Sharon and Mildred laughing about the naive tourists in Mooseville.

"*Chfff!*" The Siamese were still under the table. Yum Yum was looking for a shoelace to untie, and Koko was listening to the guests' voices with rapt concentration.

By the time the salmon croquettes were served, the host was finding it difficult to keep a dialogue alive. Junior seemed speechless with awe; no doubt he had never seen an epergne nor eaten terrine of pheasant. Roger was eating, but he seemed somewhere else. Penelope appeared preoccupied; at best her remarks were guarded, and she was not sipping her wine. As for the outspoken Amanda, she was becoming drowsier by the minute.

The waltz rhythms emanating from the foyer were soporific, Qwilleran thought, and he wished the musicians would try Mozart or Boccherini. Yet, Melinda's immediate tablemates were pleasantly animated.

In desperation he tried one subject after another. "Birch Tree's motorbike has a stereo cassette player, cruise control, and an intercom. I prefer pedaling an old-fashioned one-speed bicycle on Ittibittiwassee Road — smooth pavement, sparse traffic, and that eerie Buckshot Mine . . . You know a lot about mining history, Roger. What were the other nine mines?"

Roger blinked his eyes and said listlessly, "Well . . . there was the Goodwinter . . . and the Big B . . . and the Dimsdale."

"And the Moosejaw," his wife called out from her place farther down the table.

"The Moosejaw . . . and the Black Creek. How many is that?"

"That's only six, dear."

"Well . . . there was the Honey Hill and . . . Did I mention Old Glory?"

"Don't forget Smith's Folly, dear."

"Smith's Folly. There, that's it!" Roger concluded with relief.

Qwilleran had been counting on his fingers. "Including the Buckshot, that's only nine."

"He forgot the Three Pines," Sharon said. "That's where they had the big cave-in a few years ago. Even the *Daily Fluxion* wrote it up."

"*Chfff!*" There was another sneeze under the table.

The lamb *bûcheronne* was served, and Penelope asked, "Are you doing any writing, Mr Qwilleran?"

"Only letters. I get a tremendous amount of mail."

"I understand you answer each letter personally in a most gracious way. That's really very charming of you."

Qwilleran could hear a familiar yukking sound under the table and hoped Koko was only expressing an opinion of the conversation and not throwing up on Penelope's shoe. He could also hear Mildred, far down the table, telling Alexander about her talented art student who left town without explanation and virtually disappeared.

"A great pity," she said, "because she came from a poor family, and she could have gone to college on a scholarship and achieved some kind of success."

Alexander said with authority, "Great numbers of young women escape their humdrum existence in small towns every year, and they are assimilated into urban life, sometimes with — ah — great success. Many women professionals in New York and Washington were refugees, so to speak, from rural areas. We lose this talent because we fail to provide encouragement and opportunities and rewards."

"*Chfff!*"

"It's too bad," Mildred said, "that we don't do as much for artists as we do for farmers."

Throughout the salad course Qwilleran persevered in promoting table talk, and he was relieved when the wild raspberry trifle was served. At that point he made an announcement:

"Ladies and gentlemen, absent from this table is an important member of our household who wears many hats — those of resident manager, curator of the collection, registrar, and official appraiser. And no one has a better right to wear the hat of master chef. We are indebted to Iris Cobb for preparing this dinner tonight. I would like to ask her to join us at the table for dessert."

There were murmurs of approval as he went to the kitchen and returned with the flustered housekeeper, and there was applause when he pulled up a chair and seated Mrs Cobb between himself and Penelope. The attorney merely stiffened her spine.

When coffee and liqueurs were served in the drawing room, Qwilleran's somnolent tablemates began to revive. A few gathered in a chatty group around the life-size portrait of a young woman with a wasp waist and bustle, circa 1880.

"She was a dance-hall girl before he married her," Amanda said. "Look at that bawdy twinkle in her eye."

"Let's hear some stories, Roger," Junior urged. "Tell us about the K Saloon."

"Tell the one about Harry," Sharon suggested.

Roger had snapped out of his malaise. "Do you think I should?"

"Why not?"

"Go ahead!"

"Well, it was like this — and it's true . . . One of the regular customers at the K Saloon was a miner named Harry, and eventually he drank himself to death. He was laid out at the furniture store, which was also the undertaking parlor, and his buddies decided he should have one last night at his favorite watering hole. So they smuggled him out of the store and put him on a sledge — it was the dead of winter — and off they went to the K Saloon. They propped Harry up at the bar, and all the patrons paid their respects and drowned their grief. Finally, at three in the morning, Harry's friends put him on the sled again and whipped up the horses. They were singing and feeling no pain, so they didn't notice the corpse sliding off the tail of the icy sledge. When they got back to the furniture store — no Harry! They spent the rest of the night looking for him, but the snow was drifting and they didn't find Harry until spring."

There were gasps and groans and giggles, and Qwilleran said, "They were a bunch of necrophiliacs — that is, if the story is really true. I suspect it's apocryphal."

Penelope gave a small cough and said in a firm voice, "This has been a delightful evening, and I regret we must say good night."

Alexander said, "I emplane for Washington at an early hour tomorrow."

Amanda nudged Riker and said in a stage whisper, "They can't run the country without him."

The Mooseville group also departed. Riker drove Amanda home. Mrs Cobb went upstairs to collapse. Qwilleran and Melinda had a drink in the kitchen with the butler, the footmen, and the string trio, praising them for their performances. Then, when everyone had left, host and hostess kicked off their shoes in the library and indulged in postprandial gossip.

Melinda said, "Did you notice Penelope's reaction when you brought the cook to the table? She considered it the major faux pas of the twentieth century."

"She didn't take a drink all evening. I think she wanted champagne, but her brother vetoed it."

"Alex doesn't like her to drink; she talks too freely. How did you like her perfume, lover? It's something she asked me to bring from Paris."

"Potent, to say the least," Qwilleran said. "She was sitting on my right, you know, and I lost my sense of smell. By the time the fish was served, I couldn't taste anything. Junior was sitting next to her, and he looked glassy eyed, as if he'd been smoking something. Amanda almost passed out, and Roger couldn't remember the names of the ten defunct mines. It was the perfume, I'm sure. The cats kept sneezing."

"I had to smuggle it in," Melinda confessed. "They don't allow it to be sold in this country."

"If you ask me, it's some kind of nerve gas. What's it called?"

"Fantaisie Féline. Very expensive . . . Am I seeing things, or is that a pickax in the corner?"

"The Pickax Boosters presented it to me. I might mount it over the fireplace, or use it as a paperweight, or swing it at stray dogs when I'm biking."

At that moment Koko stalked into the library, giving Qwilleran his gimlet stare.

"By the way," Qwilleran said, "do you know anything about the Three Pines Mine?"

Melinda looked amused. "The shaft house is a notorious lovers' lair, darling. Why? Are you interested? At *your* age?"

CHAPTER TWELVE

The morning after the party Qwilleran drove Riker to the airport under threatening skies. "We're going to get the rain the farmers have been praying for and the tourist industry has been praying against."

"I hope my plane takes off before it closes in," Riker said. "Not that I'm in a hurry to get back to the *Fluxion*. I wouldn't mind living up here. Why don't you buy the *Picayune*? I'll come up here and run it for you."

"You don't mean it!"

"I do! It would be a staggering challenge."

"We'd have to fire Benjamin Franklin and spend ten million on new mechanical equipment . . . What did you think of Melinda?"

"Remarkable young woman. Does she wear green contacts? Are those her own eyelashes?"

"Everything is absolutely real," Qwilleran assured him. "I've checked it out."

"You know, Qwill, the gold diggers will be after you now. You'd be better off to marry a girl like Melinda and settle down. Her family is well-off; she has a profession; and she thinks you're tops."

"You're generous with your advice this morning." Qwilleran never liked to be told what to do.

"Okay, here's another shot. Why don't you quit hunting for the missing housemaid? You could get a bullet in the head — like the girl on the tractor."

Watching Riker's plane gain altitude, Qwilleran recalled that his friend had always tried to discourage his investigations — and had never succeeded. This time his own discretion was telling him, however, to wait for more developments before presenting the case to Chief Brodie. All he had to offer at this moment was circumstantial evidence, speculation, a sensitive moustache, and a smart cat.

Before returning home he bought a pink cashmere sweater at Lanspeak's and had it gift-wrapped. At Diamond Jim's he selected a gold necklace and dropped it off at the clinic, where a shingle at the entrance showed signs of fresh paint:

DR HALIFAX GOODWINTER, MD
DR MELINDA GOODWINTER, MD

As he approached the K mansion he was first aware of a police car, then a traffic jam, then a crowd of onlookers in the street. A bell was tolling a single solemn note as a funeral procession lined up and Tiffany's casket was carried from one of the churches on the Circle.

And then it started to rain. It rained violently, almost in anger.

Qwilleran went to his desk to write a note of condolence to Steve Trotter, with an offer of an annual scholarship in Tiffany's name. As he wrote, the telephone started to jangle with thank-you calls from the dinner guests. Junior had never eaten such good food. Sharon wanted the recipes. Mildred praised everything but thought that Alexander Goodwinter was a stuffed shirt. Amanda was hung over.

"Golly, that was a good party," the designer croaked into the phone. "I've got a hangover that would kill a horse. Did I say anything I shouldn't last night?"

"You were a model of propriety, Amanda," said Qwilleran.

"Gripes! That's the last thing I ever wanted to be. I leave that to my cousins."

"I've just driven Arch to the airport. He enjoyed your company immensely."

"He's my type! Get him up here again — soon!"

When Melinda phoned to thank him for the necklace, she complained that his line had been continually busy.

"All our dinner guests have been calling," he said. "Everyone except Penelope."

"Penny won't phone. She'll write a very proper thank-you note on engraved stationery, sealed with wax. Did Arch get away before the rains came?"

"He did, and he gave me some parting advice: (*a*) get married and (*b*) forget about the Daisy Mull mystery. I plan to take at least one of his suggestions."

At lunchtime he presented his gift to Mrs Cobb.

"Oh, Mr Qwilleran! Pink is my favorite, and I've never had anything cashmere. You shouldn't have done it. Did they all like the food last night?"

"Your dinner will make history," he assured her, "and

when you see Mrs Fulgrove, tell her that everyone admired her handwriting."

"When she was writing the place cards," Mrs Cobb said, "she told me something. I don't know whether I should repeat it."

"Go ahead." Qwilleran's remark was offhand, but his moustache was bristling with curiosity.

"Well, she works three times a week at the Goodwinter house, you know, and she overheard Miss Goodwinter and her brother having a terrible row — yelling and everything. She said it was kind of frightening because they're always so nice to each other."

"What were they arguing about?"

"She couldn't hear. She was cleaning the kitchen, and they were upstairs."

At that moment a particularly objectionable burst of music came from the upper regions of the K mansion. "I see our star boarder is still on the premises," Qwilleran said.

"He's almost finished, but his bill is going to be enormous, I'm afraid."

"Don't worry. The estate will pay for it, and I'll tell them to deduct for five breakfasts, eight lunches, seven gallons of coffee, a case of beer, and a visit to the ear doctor. I think my hearing is permanently impaired."

"Oh, Mr Qwilleran, you must be joking."

It rained hard for forty-eight hours, until the stone-paved streets of Pickax were flooded. Downtown Main Street, with its hodgepodge of architectural styles, was a parody of the Grand Canal. Grudgingly Qwilleran stayed indoors.

On the third day the rain ceased, and the wet fieldstone of the K mansion sparkled like diamonds in the sunshine. A brisk breeze started to dry up the floods. The birds sang. The Siamese rolled on the solarium floor and laundered their fur in the warm rays.

It was shortly after breakfast when an unexpected visitor arrived at the back door.

Mrs Cobb hurried to the library to find Qwilleran. "Steve Trotter is here to see you. It looks like he's had a lot to drink."

Qwilleran dropped his newspaper and went to the kitchen, where the painter in off-duty jeans and T-shirt was leaning unsteadily against the doorjamb, his face slack and his eyelids drooping.

Qwilleran pulled out two kitchen chairs. "Come in and sit down, Steve. How about a cup of coffee?"

Mrs Cobb quickly filled two mugs from the coffee maker and set them on the table, together with a plate of doughnuts.

"Don't want no coffee," Steve said, staring at Qwilleran belligerently. "Gotcha letter."

"It's hard to express the sorrow I feel about this outrageous crime," Qwilleran said. "I met Tiffany only twice, but —"

"Quit the bull! 'S all your fault," the painter said sullenly.

"I beg your pardon?"

"Y'got her mixed up in it. If y'didn't shoot off 'bout Daisy, wouldn'ta happened."

"Now wait a minute," Qwilleran said gently but firmly. "You overheard my private conversation with a visitor and went home and told your wife, didn't you? It was her idea to come here and talk about it. Furthermore, the police suspect that some tourist drove past the farm and —"

"Ain't no tourist, and y'know it."

"I haven't the least idea what you're implying, Steve."

"The letter y'sent me . . . tryin' to buy me off. No dice."

"What do you mean?"

"Y'wanna give money away to kids. Hell, what y'gonna do for me? Why'n'cha pay for the fun'ral?" With an angry gesture he swept the coffee mug off the table. It shattered on the stone floor.

Mrs Cobb made a hurried exit and returned almost immediately with Birch Tree.

"Okay, Stevie-boy," Birch said, grinning and showing his big square teeth. "Let's go home and sleep it off." He hoisted the younger man from the chair and propelled him toward the door.

Glancing out the window, Qwilleran saw the painter's truck parked with one wheel in the rhododendrons. "He can't drive in that condition," he said.

"I'll drive his truck. You follow and bring me back," Birch instructed in a tone of authority. "Only a coupla miles. Terence's dairy farm. Now you'll see where the stink comes from when the wind's from the southwest. Baa-a-a-a!"

After depositing Steve in his mobile home on the farm, Birch went to the farmhouse and talked to the in-laws. Then the two men drove back to town in the two-door, Qwilleran marveling at the man's competence and self-assurance in handling the awkward situation.

"Nice day," Birch said. "We needed rain, but they sent us too much. Baa-a-a-a!"

"I'll be able to take my bike out this afternoon," Qwilleran said.

"Me, I'm gonna knock off early and get in some fishin'. Big salmon's bitin'. a few miles off Purple Point."

"Do you have a boat?"

"Sure do. Forty-foot cruiser, loaded. Fish-finder, automatic pilot, ship-to-shore — you name it. Y'oughta get one."

Qwilleran frowned. "Fish-finder? What's that?"

"A graph, y'know. A CGR. Sonar computer graph recorder. Traces the bottom of the lake. Tells you where the fish are, and how many. First-class way to fish!"

By noontime Birch had cleared out with his noisebox and tools, and Qwilleran enjoyed his lunch in peace.

"It's good to have the doors fixed," Mrs Cobb said. "It was worth all the commotion."

Qwilleran agreed. "Now Koko won't be able to barge into my room at six a.m. He thinks everyone should get up at dawn."

The housekeeper served lunch in the cheerful breakfast room, where William and Mary banister-back chairs surrounded a dark oak table, and yellow and green chintz covered the walls and draped the windows.

"Best macaroni-and-cheese I ever tasted," Qwilleran announced.

"I found some really good cheddar at a little store behind the post office," Mrs Cobb said. After a moment she added, "I also noticed a sale of ten-speeds at the hardware store." She looked at him hopefully. "Twenty percent off."

Qwilleran grunted. "When they make a dogproof bike, I may be interested."

Later that afternoon he had another interesting scrap of conversation. The mail-cat trudged into the library to deliver Penelope's thank-you note, about which there lingered a faint but heady suggestion of Fantaisie Féline.

Qwilleran studied the intelligent-looking animal. "What was Steve trying to tell us, Koko? Who killed Tiffany Trotter — and why? And what really happened to Daisy Mull? Are we wasting our time hunting for answers?"

The cat sat tall on the desk, swaying slightly as he concentrated his blue gaze on Qwilleran's forehead. Suddenly the man realized that Koko had never experienced the murals in Daisy's apartment. He grabbed him and carried him out to the garage. The sleek body was neither struggling in protest nor limp with acquiescence — just taut with anticipation.

First Koko was allowed to examine the cars, the bicycle, the garden implements. It was always better to let him take his time and follow his own inclinations. Eventually he found the flight of stairs and scampered up to the living quarters. In the freshly painted apartment he craned his neck and sniffed in every direction without any apparent pleasure. Then he wandered down the hall and into the jungle of daisies.

Koko's first reaction was to flatten himself, belly to

the floor. All around him were wild, tangled, threatening forms on walls and ceiling. Cats could not distinguish colors, Qwilleran had been told, but they could sense them. When Koko concluded that the place was safe, he started slinking around, inspecting with caution several mysterious spots on the rug, a scratch on the dresser, and a rip in the chair upholstery. As his investigation reassured him, he stretched to his full length before prancing around the room in a dance of exhilaration — as if he could hear music in colors that Qwilleran could appreciate only with his eyes.

Then something unseen alerted the cat. He looked quickly this way and that, ran a few steps, jumped and waved his paw, scurried across the room, turned and leaped through the air, twisting his lithe body into a back somersault.

Remembering Mrs Cobb's haunted-house theory, Qwilleran shivered involuntarily until he realized the truth. It was almost August, the season of houseflies, and Koko was chasing a tiny flying insect, matching its aerial swooping with his own acrobatics. He chased it into the hallway and soon returned, chomping and licking his chops.

"Disgusting!" Qwilleran told him. "Is that all you can find to do?"

Koko was excited by the chase and the kill, and he was bent on finding another prey. He jumped onto the bed and stood on his hind legs, extending a paw up the wall. He was a yard long when he stretched to the limit. He pawed the graffiti, trying to reach one set of initials nestled in the pattern of hearts, flowers, and foliage.

Then he sprang, and a fly fell down behind the bed. In a split second the cat was after it. Dead or alive, the fly had fallen between the mattress and the wall. Koko reached into the crevice with one slender foreleg and then the other, mumbling to himself in determined gutturals.

Qwilleran watched the struggle for a while before pulling the bed away from the wall. Like a hawk Koko dived into the aperture, and soon there were sounds of moist chomping.

"Revolting!" Qwilleran said. "You eat those filthy flies, but you won't eat catfood with added vitamins and minerals. Let's get out of here. We're going home."

Koko remained behind the bed. "*Chfff! Chfff!*" It was that delicate cat-sneeze.

"It's dusty back there! Get out! Let's go!"

The cat failed to respond, and Qwilleran felt the old tingling sensation on his upper lip. Once before, Koko had dredged up some telling mementoes from behind a bed. Kneeling on the mattress the man peered down into the shadows. Koko was hunched over something, sniffing it, nuzzling it, poking it with one inquisitive paw.

Qwilleran reached down and retrieved a notebook — a school notebook with torn and ruffled pages. Koko immediately jumped out of his hiding place, yowling and demanding his treasure. Some of the pages had obviously been nibbled by mice.

With the notebook in one hand and the indignant cat in the other, Qwilleran returned to the house and headed for the library. Koko was howling in high dudgeon, and Yum Yum came running from the solarium, shrieking in sympathy. She was followed by Mrs Cobb. "What's the matter? What's going on here?"

"Give them a treat, will you? Get them out of my hair!"

"Treat!" she cried, and led the way to the kitchen like the Pied Piper.

Qwilleran closed the library door and settled down to inspect Koko's find. It was the cheapest kind of notebook, with ruled pages, some of them nibbled and all of them stained. It had a definite mousy odor.

"A diary!" he said aloud, as he thumbed through the soiled pages with distaste. He could distinguish dates, but the handwriting was completely illegible. Once upon a time he had known an artist who could make every letter of the alphabet look like a *U*; Daisy made every letter look like *O*. The cursive writing was a coil of overlapping circles. The art teacher's comment had been apt; Daisy's calligraphic invention was attractive to the eye but impossible to read.

After his bike ride, he decided, he would phone Mildred Hanstable and ask her to look at the diary — and translate it if possible. Meanwhile he added it to the growing collection in the desk drawer: the ivory elephant, a gold bracelet, a postal card, and an envelope with a thousand in cash.

Every one of these memorabilia had been found by that phenomenal cat, he recalled. Yet Koko always made his discoveries seem so casual. This time he went through the motions of chasing a fly, pursuing it up the wall, batting it down as it tried to camouflage itself among the initials . . . What were the initials?

Qwilleran made a dash to the garage and back. Grabbing the little telephone directory, he combed two columns of listings. Only three subscribers had the right initials: Sam Gafner, Scott Gippel, and Senior Goodwinter.

If SC had been the object of Daisy's affection, it would have to be Gafner, he concluded. Scott Gippel was the enormous councilman who required two chairs. Junior's father — with his paper hat and bemused expression — would hardly appeal to a giddy young girl. Gafner, the real estate broker, was the most likely candidate. After his bike ride, he decided, he would do some serious research.

It was a beautiful day for biking. Warmed by the sun and caressed by light breezes, Qwilleran headed for his favorite country road. The vegetation, freshly washed, was a vibrant green. Flocks of blackbirds rose from the brush and followed the lone rider, scolding with staccato chirps. Clicks in the sprocket and rear wheel added to the chorus. He remembered Mrs Cobb's parting words: "Be careful with that broken-down contraption, Mr Q. You really ought to buy a ten-speed."

Everything on Ittibittiwassee Road smelled damp and clean. The sun and breezes had dried the pavement, but the roadside ditch was filled with rainwater. It was a good thirty feet from the pavement to allow for future widening of the road. This would be a major highway when the condominium development was completed. Too bad! He liked the quiet and the loneliness of the road.

Coming up on the right was the site of the old Buckshot Mine, where miners had died in a cave-in in 1913. As he pedaled past the ruins he listened intently for the eerie whistling sound said to emanate from the mineshaft. The abandoned shaft house, a weathered silver, had been drenched with rain.

Qwilleran was studying the ruins with such concentration that he was unaware of a truck approaching from the opposite direction — unaware until its motor roared. He looked ahead in time to see its burst of speed, its sudden swerve into the eastbound lane, a murderous monster bearing down upon him and his rickety bicycle. He yanked the handlebars and plunged down toward the ditch, but his front wheel hit a rock, and he went sailing over the handlebars. For an interminable moment he was airborne . . .

When he climbed out of the ditch, dazed and wet and bleeding, he staggered painfully to the deserted highway, not knowing where he was or why he was there.

Roads go somewhere. Follow the road. Move. Keep moving.

In a few minutes or a few hours a car stopped. A man jumped out, shouting, and put him in the front seat. For a few minutes — or hours — he sat in a speeding car. The man kept shouting.

What is he saying? I don't know — I can't —

He was wheeled into a building. Bright lights. Strange people, talking, talking — He was tired.

The next morning he opened his eyes and found himself in a strange bed in a strange room.

CHAPTER THIRTEEN

Before Qwilleran was released from Pickax Hospital, he had a consultation with Dr Melinda.

"All your tests turned out fine," she said. "You're a very healthy guy — for your age."

"And for a young chick you're a very smart doctor."

"I'm so smart, lover, that I sneaked in a Wassermann test in case you want to apply for a marriage license. I'm also writing you a prescription for a crash helmet. With your head injury you could have drowned in that drainage ditch."

"I'm sure the hit-runner thought he was leaving me for dead."

"Some strange things are happening in Moose County," Melinda said. "Amanda may be right about the tourist invasion. You should report it to the police."

"On the strength of what? My dream? Brodie would think I damaged something else besides my bicycle. No, Melinda, I'm merely going to keep a sharp lookout for a certain truck. In my dream I could see it clearly, coming at me fast, a rusty grille grinning at me, towering over me. It was one of those terrain vehicles."

"Junior was one scared kid when he brought you in. He thought you were a zombie."

"It was a strange experience, Melinda. When I opened my eyes in a hospital bed and didn't know where I was or *who* I was, it didn't disturb me at all. It was simply a puzzle that aroused my curiosity. Glad you got Arch Riker up here to straighten me out."

Riker picked Qwilleran up at the hospital in a rental car from the airport. "I have time for a cuppa, Qwill, before I catch my plane."

"Then head north at the traffic light and we'll tune in the coffee hour at the Dismal Diner. If you think the Press Club is a gossip mill, wait till you hear the boys up here."

"What did your tests show? Everything okay?"

"Everything's fine, but I have some ugly suspicions about my bike mishap. It was no accident, Arch! It was a hit-run attempt on my life."

"I warned you! Why do you get mixed up in criminal investigations that are none of your business? Leave it to the authorities."

"This has nothing to do with the missing housemaid. It's something else entirely. I came to that conclusion when I was lying in that hospital bed. You know the conditions of the Klingenschoen bequest: I have to live in Pickax for five years or the estate goes to a syndicate in New Jersey. Well, what happens if I *die* before the five years are up?"

"Without knowing anything about probate law," Riker said, "I'd guess that the dough goes to New Jersey."

"So it's to their advantage if I fade out before the five years are up. In fact, the sooner the better."

Riker gave his passenger an incredulous glance.

"That's a jarring thought, Qwill. Why do you suspect them?"

"It's a so-called foundation involved in some dubious venture in Atlantic City. I don't trust those people."

The editor said, "When I first heard about the Old Lady's will, I knew it was too good to be true. Forget the inheritance, Qwill. You never wanted a fortune anyway. You know you can have your job back at the *Fluxion*."

"Then the money will leave Moose County."

"Don't try to be a hero. Get out of here and save your skin. Let those forty-two affluent Goodwinters buy some new books for the library."

Qwilleran lingered his moustache with uncertainty. "I'll figure out something. I've got an appointment with the attorney this afternoon. And maybe we'll hear some scuttlebutt at the diner."

The coffee hour was effervescing in a haze of blue smoke. A few men in feed caps nodded to Qwilleran as he and Riker helped themselves to coffee and doughnuts. The two newsmen sat at a side table, listening.

"He's handin' out cigars, but he ain't the father."

"I butcher my own hogs, make my own sausage. Only way to go."

"It says in the Bible that a fool's voice is known by its multitude of words, and that fits him all right!"

"Birds! That's my bag, and I always limit out."

"If she's a lawyer, why would she want to get married?"

"They had to shoot the whole herd. Damn shame!"

"All she wants is his dough, I betcha."

"Man, my wife makes the best rabbit stew you ever tasted."

"Never heard the name. Is it Russian or something?"

"My mother-in-law's been here goin' on three weeks."

Before heading for the airport Riker dropped Qwilleran off at his house. "Did you get any clues from all that bull?" he asked.

Qwilleran shook his head. "They know who I am. They clammed up."

If he was expecting a joyous welcome from the Siamese, he was disappointed. They could smell the hospital, and they circled him with distaste, Yum Yum hissing and Koko producing a chesty rumble that sounded like distant thunder. The situation was still a standoff when he left for his one o'clock appointment.

He walked into the law office slowly, still hampered by the wrappings on his sutured knee. Penelope also lacked her usual verve. She was wearing dark glasses and looking pale. In a shaky voice she said, "You look a trifle battered, Mr Qwilleran, but we are all thankful it was no worse. What can I do for you?"

He stated his question about the Klingenschoen will.

"As you know," Penelope reminded him, "it was a holographic will. The dear lady insisted on writing it herself, without an attorney and without witnesses, to protect her privacy. Let me review the document again to refresh my memory."

The clerk brought the handwritten will, and Penelope read it carefully, shaking her head. "You are justified in being concerned. In the event of your death the estate would go to the alternate heirs in New Jersey. But surely you have nothing to worry about. Except for your temporary injuries, you seem extraordinarily healthy."

"Then brace yourself," Qwilleran said. He repeated his suspicion about the so-called accident and his distrust of the East Coast heirs. "Is there anyone in town who comes from that part of the country or has connections there?"

"Not to my knowledge," she said, looking pensive and withdrawn.

He refrained from mentioning his private list of suspects. Hackpole had worked in Newark. The gardener was a Princeton man. Qwilleran's own former in-laws — an obnoxious crew — pursued some questionable profession in the Garden State.

To the attorney he said, "In any event I feel strongly that the money should stay in Moose County. It belongs here, and it can do a lot of good. How can we circumvent the present situation? Are there any loopholes? May I write a will myself, assigning my claim to the Klingenschoen Foundation?"

"I'm afraid not," Penelope said. "The language of the original will fails to grant you that power . . . Let me think . . . This is really an unfortunate development, Mr Qwilleran. I can only hope you are wrong in your suspicions."

"Then be advised," he said, "that I'm going to write the will anyway. If anything happens to me, you'd better demand an investigation into the cause of my death."

"I must say, Mr Qwilleran, you are very calm and businesslike about a distressing possibility."

"I've been in hot spots before," he said, waving her comment aside. "I'll write a holographic will, so Goodwinter & Goodwinter cannot be faulted for giving me bad advice. And I'll see that all the bases are covered — the police, the prosecutor's office, the media . . ."

"What can I say? . . . Except that I'm quite upset about your allegations."

"So be it. Discuss it with your brother, if you see fit, but right or wrong, that's going to be my course of action."

As he hobbled from the office he thought, She's hung over; she needs a hair of the dog. So he hobbled back into Penelope's presence. "Your rain check is still good, Miss Goodwinter. I'd like to suggest cocktails and dinner at the Old Stone Mill tonight, if you don't mind dining with a walking accident statistic."

She hesitated briefly before saying, "Thank you, Mr Qwilleran, but not tonight, I'm afraid."

Her telltale physiological condition surprised him more than her refusal of his invitation. Regarding the latter he decided she just didn't like frozen ravioli.

At breakfast the next morning Mrs Cobb had more Goodwinter gossip to report.

"Sorry to be late," Qwilleran apologized as he sat down to a plate of real buttermilk pancakes and real Canadian peameal bacon. "I seem to require more sleep since my accident." He sniffed critically. "I smell lavender."

"That's English wax," the housekeeper said. "Mrs Fulgrove is working on the dining room furniture." She tiptoed to the door of the breakfast room and closed it gently. "She told me the Goodwinters had another fight when he got home from Washington. Miss G was shouting about mosquitoes — and a woman — and a dead body, whatever that means. None of it was very clear to me. Mrs Fulgrove is hard to understand. She also said something about a *cow* opening a restaurant in Pickax."

"It can't be any worse than the restaurants we've got," he said. "It might even be better. Any phone calls?"

"Lori Bamba called. She said her husband will drop off the first batch of letters for you to sign. Mrs Hanstable phoned to say she's picking wild blueberries and asked if we wanted any. She sells them to raise money for the hospital."

"I hope you placed an order."

"I told her two quarts. She'll drop them off tomorrow when she comes in town to have her hair done."

"You women," he said, "structure your lives around your hair appointments."

"Oh, Mr Q," she laughed, admonishing him with her eyes. She was acting girlish, he thought, and he soon found out why. "I've been invited out to dinner tonight," she said. "A man I met at the Historical Society."

"Good! I'll grab a hamburger somewhere."

"You don't need to do that, Mr Qwilleran. I bought four beautiful loin chops and some big Idaho bakers, and I could put them in the oven before I go. I thought maybe you'd like to ask someone over."

"Good idea! I'll invite Junior. I owe him one."

In the afternoon Nick Bamba arrived with seventy-five

beautifully typed letters. He said proudly, "Lori makes each reply a little different, so it won't seem like a form letter. She's good at writing."

Qwilleran liked the young engineer from Mooseville. He had a healthy head of black curly hair and eyes like black onyx that shone with enthusiasm, and he always had some choice tidbit of information to impart.

"Glad you weren't seriously hurt, Qwill. Lori was praying for you."

"Tell her I need all the prayers I can get. How's she feeling?"

"Okay, except mornings, but that's natural."

"Would you like a beer?"

"Got anything stronger? Lori's on the wagon for the duration, so I do my drinking away from home."

"Spoken like a considerate husband," Qwilleran remarked.

They sat in the solarium with their drinks and discussed the Trotter case, bicycles, dogs, and the coffee crowd at the Dimsdale Diner.

"On the way down here," Nick said, "I stopped at the diner for lunch, and I saw something unusual. Is Alex Goodwinter your attorney?"

"Actually his sister is handling the estate."

"I hear she's pretty sharp. I wish I could say the same for Alex. He gave a talk to the Mooseville Boosters a while back, and he's the dullest speaker I ever heard. He makes a good appearance, and a good presentation, but when it's all over, what has he said? Nothing!"

"What happened at the diner?" Qwilleran asked casually, although his curiosity was rampant.

"I was sitting at a window table, eating some by-product of a sawmill called meatloaf, and I saw this Cadillac pull into the parking lot. Usually it's all pickups and vans, you know."

"You mean you could actually see through the dirt on those windows?"

"Lori says I can see through a brick wall."

"So what did you see?"

"It was Alex driving the Caddie, and he sat there at the wheel with the motor running until one of the owners of the place went out and got in the front seat with him."

"Which partner?" Qwilleran asked.

"Not the cook. The big husky one who rides around on a motorbike. The two of them sat in the car, and it looked like they were arguing. Finally Alex got out his wallet and counted out some bills. I'd like to know what that little deal was all about."

Qwilleran's suspicions were piqued, but he offered a matter-of-fact explanation. "The guy does maintenance work. Alex could have been settling an account."

"In cash? Why wouldn't he write a check?" Nick leaned forward in his chair. "You know, I've always thought they were selling something besides food at the diner. Otherwise, how could that dump stay in business?"

Qwilleran chose to taunt Nick. "Alex is a leading citizen, a pillar of the community, a genuine rockbound Goodwinter. How can you cast aspersions?"

"Alex is a genuine four-flusher," said Nick, getting a little heated. "He likes to make people think he's an important influence in Washington, but I say he's down there having a good time."

"What does Lori think about him?"

"You know women!" Nick said with disdain. "She thinks he's a dreamboat — that's her word for him. I have another word."

Nick left, taking fifty more letters for his wife to answer, and Qwilleran visited the hardware store to look at bicycles. When he returned he said to Mrs Cobb, "Do you know what they're asking for a ten-speed? More than I paid for my first car!"

"But you can afford it, Mr Q."

"That's not the point . . . You look very nice this afternoon, Mrs Cobb."

"Thank you. I had my hair done." She was wearing more makeup than usual. "You'll never guess who invited me to dinner tonight! It's that man who objected to the forty-eight star flag."

"What? Hackpole?"

"Herb Hackpole. He's really very nice. He runs a garage, and he's going to find out why my van drips oil."

Qwilleran huffed into his moustache and reserved comment.

While waiting for Junior to arrive, he prepared dinner for the Siamese. Yum Yum had forgiven him for smelling like a hospital and had even jumped onto his lap and touched his moustache with an inquisitive paw. It was one of her endearing gestures. Accustomed to stealing toothbrushes and paintbrushes, she had never been able to understand bristles attached to a face.

Koko, on the other hand, was giving Qwilleran the silent treatment. He had stopped hissing and growling but regarded the man with utter contempt. When the plate of boned chicken was placed on the floor, he refused to eat until Qwilleran had left the room. It was an attitude entirely without precedent.

Junior arrived promptly at six, with the ravenous hunger of a twenty-two-year-old. "Hey, you look good in bandages, Qwill. You ought to wear them all the time."

They ate their pork chops at the massive kitchen table. "According to Mrs Cobb," Qwilleran pointed out, "this is probably a sixteenth-century table from a Spanish monastery."

"She's a swell cook," Junior said. "You're lucky."

"She made a fresh peach pie for our dessert . . . Have another roll, Junior. They're sourdough . . . She went to dinner tonight with a guy from the Historical Society. I hope he's a decent sort. She's gullible, and I feel responsible, since I brought her up here from Down Below. Do you know Herb Hackpole?"

Junior finished chewing a large mouthful. "Everybody knows that guy."

"Mrs Cobb finds him quite likable."

"Oh sure. He can be likable if he wants something. Mostly he's a troublemaker, always calling the paper with some piddling complaint, and we can't get kids to deliver papers on his block because of his dogs . . . Pass the butter, Qwill."

"Has he always lived here?"

"Born and raised here, Dad says. In school everybody

hated his guts. He was your standard small-town bully, you know. The whole town cheered when he went east to work. Too bad he came back . . . Is there another beer?"

"Sure, and we've got a couple more ears of corn in the pot."

Over coffee and peach pie the young editor said, "I'm supposed to ask you a favor. Do you know the secretary at G&G? She's my aunt."

"I noticed a family resemblance," Qwilleran said.

"She thinks Penny is headed for trouble — working long hours and worried about something and *drinking*, which she doesn't usually do. My aunt thought maybe you could talk her into taking a vacation — a health spa in Mexico, or something like that."

"Me? I'm only a client. She won't even go to lunch with me."

"But Penny admires you a lot, no kidding. She used to clip your columns when you were writing for the *Fluxion*. She always —" He was interrupted abruptly by the insistent sound of his beeper. He jumped up and ran to the door. "Sorry. There's a fire. Great meal!"

He barreled away in his red Jaguar as the siren at City Hall summoned the volunteer firefighters.

It had been a busy day for Qwilleran, and it was not yet over. Penelope Goodwinter phoned to ask if she could pay a visit and bring a bottle.

CHAPTER FOURTEEN

In preparation for Penelope's visit Qwilleran carried an ice bucket and other bar essentials to the library. That was when he noticed several books on the floor — part of a twelve-volume set. The morocco covers were splayed and the India paper pages crumpled. His eyes traveled upward to the shelf and found Koko squeezed into the space between volumes II and VIII, having a nap. He had always liked to sleep on bookshelves.

"Bad cat!" Qwilleran shouted as he examined the mistreated books.

Waking suddenly, Koko yawned, stretched, and jumped to the floor, and stalked out of the room without comment.

Qwilleran replaced the books carefully, and at the same time he wondered if anyone in that house had ever read the handsomely bound twelve-volume poem titled *Doomsday*.

Doomsday! Qwilleran thought. Is that a prediction or some kind of catly curse?

He expected the tan BMW to pull into the circular drive as usual. Instead, the headlights searched out the rear of the house, and Penelope knocked at the back door with a playful rat-tat-tat that was out of keeping with her accustomed reserve.

"I hope you don't mind my coming to the service entrance," she caroled, waving a bottle of fine old Scotch. "After all, this is a terribly informal call."

She was relaxed almost to the point of gaiety, and she looked casual and comfortable in white ducks, sandals, and a navy blue jersey. As Melinda had mentioned, a little nip did wonders for Penelope's personality. Yet, her face was haggard and her eyes looked tired. One earring was missing, and she wore no perfume.

"The ice cubes await us in the library," Qwilleran said with a flourish. "I find it the friendliest room in the house."

The brown tones of bookbindings and leather upholstery absorbed the lamplight, producing a seductive glow. Penelope slid into the slippery leather sofa and crossed her knees with the grace of a long-legged woman. Qwilleran chose a lounge chair and propped his injured leg on an ottoman.

"Are you on the mend?" she asked in a solicitous tone that sounded genuine.

"Twenty-three of my stitches are beginning to itch," he said, "so that's a healthy sign. I'm glad you decided to take a break. You've been working much too hard."

"I admit my eyes are weary."

"You need a couple of wet tea bags," he said. "My mother always recommended wet tea bags for tired eyes."

"Is the remedy effective?"

"Now is an appropriate time to find out." He hoisted

himself out of the chair and returned with two soggy tea bags on a Wedgwood saucer. "Rest your head on the back of the sofa."

She slid into a loungy position and said, "Oooh!" as he pressed the tea bags on her closed eyelids.

"How long since you've had a vacation, Penelope? I'm tired of calling you Miss Goodwinter. From now on it's *Penelope* whether you like it or not."

"I like it," she murmured.

"You should take a sybaritic week or two at one of those expensive health resorts," he suggested.

"A cruise would be more to my liking. Do you like cruise ships, Mr Qwilleran?"

"I can't say I've ever sailed strictly for pleasure . . . And it's *Qwill*, Penelope. Please!"

"Now that you're a man of leisure, you might try it — the Greek islands, the Norwegian fjords —" She was waving an empty glass in his direction, and Qwilleran poured a refill. Her first drink had disappeared fast.

"Before I start goofing off and taking cruises, I hope to produce a literary masterpiece or two," he said.

"You have a wonderful writing style. I always enjoyed your column in the *Fluxion*. You were so clever when you were writing on a subject you knew nothing about."

"Trick of the trade," he said modestly.

"It was once my ambition to be a writer, but you have real talent, Qwill. I could never aspire to what you seem to do with the greatest of ease."

Qwilleran knew he was a good writer, but he liked enormously to be told so, especially by an attractive woman. While one half of his mind basked in her effusive compliments, the other half was wondering why she had come. Had she argued with her brother again and escaped his surveillance? Why did he supervise her social conduct so assiduously? How could a stuffed shirt like Alexander exert so much influence over this intelligent woman?

Penelope was being unusually agreeable. She inquired about the health of the Siamese, Amanda's progress with the redecorating, and Mrs Cobb's cataloguing of the collection.

"Her most recent discovery," Qwilleran said, "is a pair of majolica vases that had been relegated to the attic — circa 1870 and now worth thousands. They're just outside the door here — on top of another valuable item that she found in the garage — a Pennsylvania German wardrobe. She calls it a *Schrank*. Seven feet high, and Koko can sail to the top of it in a single effortless leap."

Qwilleran wondered whether she was listening. He had spent enough time at cocktail parties to know the rhythm of social drinking, and Penelope was exceeding the speed limit. She was also sliding farther down on the slippery sofa.

In a kindly voice he said, "Be careful! The drinks can hit you hard when you're tired. You've been spending too many long hours at the office. Is it really worth it?"

"A junior partner," she said hesitantly, "has to keep her grind to the nosestone." She giggled. "Nose . . . to the . . . grindstone."

Qwilleran slipped into an investigative role he had played many times — helpful and sympathetic, but somewhat devious. "It must be gratifying, Penelope, to know that your brother is accomplishing so much for the county when he spends his valuable time in Washington. It's a worthwhile sacrifice that he's making. I understand that he made a speech recently to the Mooseville Boosters, and they're still talking about it."

Penelope discarded the tea bags and struggled to her feet, in order to pour a more generous drink of Scotch for herself. "Did he tell them about his social — his social — conquests down there?" Her voice had a bitter edge, and her tongue tangled with certain words. "It's not — not all — business, you know."

"No doubt he'll run for office one of these days," Qwilleran went on, "and then his social contacts will be useful."

Penelope stared at him through a fog and spoke slowly and carefully. "Alex couldn't . . . get elected . . . mayor of . . . Dimsdale."

"You don't mean that, Penelope. With his name and background and suave manner and striking appearance he'd be a knockout in politics. He'd make a hit with the media. That's what counts these days."

Nastiness and alcohol contorted her handsome features. "He couldn't . . . get anywhere . . . without me." Her eyes were not focusing, and when she put her glass down on the table, it missed the edge. "Sorry," she said as she scrambled about on her knees, picking up ice cubes.

Qwilleran was relentless. "I'm sure you could manage the office efficiently while the senior partner is doing great things in the Capitol."

The brilliant, articulate Penelope was pathetically struggling to make sense. "He won't . . . go down there. He'll bring . . . he'll bring her . . . up here. New partner!"

Remarks overheard at the Dimsdale Diner flashed through Qwilleran's mind. "Is she an attorney?"

Penelope gulped what remained of her melted ice cubes. "Bring her . . . into the firm, that's what . . . but over my . . . dead body! I . . . won't . . . have it. *Won't have it!*"

"Penelope," he said soothingly, "it will be a good thing for you. Another partner will relieve you of some of the pressure."

She uttered a hysterical laugh. "Goodwinter, Goodwinter & Sh- Smfska!" She stumbled over the name. "Goodwinter, Goodwinter & Smfska! We'll be . . . laughingstock . . . of the county!"

"Have you expressed your feelings to your brother? Perhaps he'll reconsider."

She was losing control. "He'll . . . he'll marry . . . he'll marry that — that tramp! But I'll . . . I'll stop it. I can . . . stop it. *Stop it!*" She looked wild-eyed and disheveled. "I feel . . . awful!"

Qwilleran pulled her to her feet. "You need fresh air." He walked her to the solarium and through the French doors and held her sympathetically while she gave vent to tears. "Do you want black coffee, Penelope?"

She shook her head.

"Shall I take you home?"

He drove the BMW to the turreted stone residence on Goodwinter Boulevard, with Penelope crumpled on the seat beside him. He parked under the porte cochere and carried her up the steps to the carriage entrance. A housekeeper came running, and Alexander appeared in a silk dressing gown.

"She's not well," Qwilleran said. "I think she's overly tired."

Alexander looked at his sister sternly and without compassion. "Take her upstairs," he told the housekeeper. Turning to Qwilleran he said, "Where did you — ah — find her?"

"She came to the house to discuss a legal matter, and she was taken ill. I think she needs a rest — a vacation — before she has a breakdown. Put her in the hospital for a few days. She should have a checkup."

"It is unfortunate," Alexander said, "but she goes completely out of her head when she touches alcohol, and she speaks the most utter nonsense. Thank you for returning her — ah — safely. Allow me to drive you home."

"No thanks. It's only a short distance, and it's a nice night."

As he walked slowly through the moonlit streets he reflected that Mrs Fulgrove's report about "mosquitoes" and a dead body was roughly related to the facts, and he concluded that Penelope was overreacting to the threat of Ms Smfska as professional partner and future sister-in-law. True, it would generate merriment in Moose County, especially among the coffee-shop regulars. Anyone familiar with the Goodwinter mystique and Penelope's insufferable snobbery would be amused at the thought of Goodwinter, Goodwinter & Smfska.

Among the cackling, bleating, guffawing crowd at the Dismal Diner it would probably become Goodwinter, Goodwinter & Mosquito. Nevertheless, after hospital rest and a vacation, he decided, the junior partner would regain her perspective.

Approaching the K mansion, he glanced at the second floor. The lights were turned on in Mrs Cobb's suite, indicating that she had returned safely after an evening with that ape! She had always been attracted to tattoos and crew cuts. Her late husband had been a brutish-looking ruffian.

There was a light in the back entry, but the rest of the service area was dark, and as Qwilleran unlocked the door he heard a scraping sound in the kitchen. He stood motionless and listened intently, trying to identify it. *Scrape* . . . pause . . . *long scrape* . . . pause . . . *two short scrapes*. He crossed the stone floor silently in his deck shoes, reached inside the kitchen door, and flicked on the lights.

There in the middle of the floor was the cats' heavy metal commode filled with kitty gravel, and behind it was Koko, preparing to give it another shove with his nose. The cat looked up with startled eyes and ears.

"You bad cat!" Qwilleran said sharply. "You're the one who's been moving things around! You could kill a person! Cut it out!"

He returned the commode to the laundry room and went upstairs to think about Penelope and compare her to Melinda. They were both handsome women with the Goodwinter features and intelligence and education. The attorney was the more striking of the two, but she lacked

Melinda's equanimity and sense of humor. He was lucky to have a healthy, well-adjusted woman like Melinda who called him "lover" and managed great dinner parties and knew how to pronounce sphygmomanometer.

The next morning he found Mildred Hanstable in the kitchen delivering wild blueberries. She and Mrs Cobb were having a cup of coffee and getting acquainted.

Qwilleran said, "Mildred, you'll be interested to know that Mrs Cobb is a palmist."

Mildred squealed with delight. "Really? Would you be willing to read palms at the hospital bazaar? We have tarot card readings and raise quite a bit of money that way."

The housekeeper seemed flattered. "I'd be glad to, if you think I'm good enough."

Diplomatically Qwilleran steered Mildred out of the kitchen and into the library, where he seated her in a comfortable chair and handed her a grubby clutch of yellowed paper.

She shuddered and recoiled. "What's that?"

"Daisy's diary. We found it behind her bed. It's totally illegible. I can distinguish a date at the top of each page, that's all. She began writing January first and ended in May."

Mildred accepted the diary gingerly. "It looks like a mouse nest, but it's her handwriting, all right. I wonder if I can decipher it." She studied the first page. "Once you get the hang of her letter formation it's not so bad . . . Let's see. It starts with 'Happy New Year to me,' but the spelling's atrocious . . . Hmmm . . . She says her mother is drunk. Poor girl never knew what it was to have a decent parent . . . She mentions Rick. They go out in the woods and throw snowballs at trees. He buys her a burger . . . How'm I doing, Qwill?"

"You're amazing! Don't stop."

"Oh-oh! On January second she loses her job at the studio. Calls Amanda a witch. There's something about an elephant, spelled with an *f*. It's a Christmas present from Rick."

"He's the one who stole it," Qwilleran guessed. "Amanda blamed Daisy. Her friends used to hang around the studio."

Mildred scanned the pages. "Very depressing . . . until January fifteenth. She gets a job at the Goodwinter house — uniforms provided. A room of her own. Won't have to live with Della. She celebrates with Rick, Ollie, Tiff and Jim."

"Tiffany is the one who was shot on her father's farm."

"Yes, I know. I had her in home ec. Married one of the Trotter boys. Father injured in a tractor accident . . . Now the diary skips to February. Daisy decides she doesn't like housework. Well, neither do I, to tell the truth . . . A new boyfriend, Sandy, gives her cologne for a Valentine. Spelled *k-l-o-n-e*. See what I mean about her spelling? . . . She doesn't write much in March . . . April is pretty well messed up . . . Oh-oh! Lost her job again."

"That's when she started working here, according to the employment records," Qwilleran said.

"She's in love with Sandy, spelled *l-u-v* . . . No more mention of Rick or Ollie or Jim . . . Sounds as if she's serious. Sandy gives her a gold bracelet . . . Let's see what else . . . Oh-oh! Here — on April thirteenth — she thinks she's pregnant . . . Tiff takes her to Dr Hal . . . Very happy now . . . She sketches some wedding dresses . . . Della is pleased. Knits some things for the baby . . . Now there are pages torn out . . . April thirtieth, she cries all night. Sandy wants her to have an abortion. No marriage . . . He gives her money . . . Della tells her to have the baby and make him pay . . . That's all. That's the last entry."

"Sad story, but it confirms all our guesses."

"Where can I wash my hands, Qwill? This book is foul. And I have to go and get my hair done."

After escorting Mildred to her car, he returned to the library to lock up the diary. To his surprise the desk drawer was open. He was sure he had closed it, but now it stood a few inches ajar. The ivory elephant was there — and the gold bracelet — and the postal card. But the envelope of money had vanished.

He made a quick trip to the kitchen, where Mrs Cobb was preparing mustard sauce for the smoked tongue. "Was anyone here in the last half hour?"

"Only Mrs Hanstable."

"I accompanied her to her car, and when I returned, my desk drawer was open, and an important envelope was missing."

"I can't imagine, unless . . . I told you strange things have been going on in this house, Mr Q."

He headed back to the library to make a thorough search of his desktop — just in time to see Koko plodding aimlessly through the foyer, his jaws clamped on the corner of a white envelope that dragged between his legs.

"Drop that!" Qwilleran shouted. "Bad cat! How did you get it?"

Koko dropped the envelope, stepped over it with unconcern, and went to sit on the third stair of the staircase.

In the library Qwilleran found scratches on the front edge of the drawer. It was a heavy drawer, and Koko had gone to some trouble to open it. Why?

Ever since the accident on Ittibittiwassee Road, Koko had been acting strangely. Prior to that episode he and Qwilleran had been good companions. They treated each other as equals. The man talked to the cat, and the cat listened and blinked and looked wise, then answered with a "yow" that signified tolerant interest or hearty agreement or violent disapproval. They had played games together, and since moving into the K mansion Koko had been particularly attentive.

Suddenly all that had changed. Koko's attitude was one of scornful aloofness, and he committed annoying misdemeanors — like pushing his commode around the kitchen, knocking fine books off the shelf, and — now — stealing money. Something was wrong. A personality change in an animal usually signified illness, yet Koko was the acme of health. His eyes sparkled; his appetite was good; his lithe body was taut with energy; he romped with Yum Yum. Only with Qwilleran was he reserved and remote.

There were no ready answers, and Koko committed no further mischief that day, but late that night

Qwilleran was reading in his upstairs sitting room when he heard prolonged wailing, shrill and mournful. Hurrying downstairs as fast as the injured knee would permit, he followed the eerie sound to the back of the house. There, in a shaft of moonlight that beamed into the solarium, was an alarming performance. Koko, his fur unnaturally ruffled, was half crouched, with his head thrown back, and he was howling an unearthly lament that made the blood run cold.

The tall case clock in the foyer bonged twice. Approaching the cat cautiously, Qwilleran spoke to him in a soothing voice and then stroked his ridged fur until he calmed down.

"You're a good cat, Koko, and a good friend," Qwilleran said, "and I'm sorry if I've been preoccupied or cross. You've been trying to get my attention. You're smarter than I am sometimes, and I should read your messages instead of flying off on a wild hunch. Will you forgive me? Can we be friends again? You and Yum Yum are all the family I've got."

Koko blinked his eyes and squeaked a faint "ik ik ik."

It was two o'clock. Four hours later Qwilleran found out what it was all about.

CHAPTER FIFTEEN

It was six o'clock, but Qwilleran already was awake when the telephone startled him with its early-morning ring of urgency. His curiosity had been working overtime and disturbing his sleep ever since Penelope's unexpected visit and Koko's unexplained antics. Was the nocturnal howl a protest? A warning? Or was it something that cats do in the light of a full moon?

Then the telephone rang, and a familiar voice said in an ominous minor key, "Qwill, did I wake you? I thought you'd want to know — Penelope has taken her life!"

He was stunned into silence.

"Qwill, this is Melinda."

"I know. I heard you. I can't believe it! Yes, I *can* believe it. I knew she was on the brink of something. What a bloody shame! What a waste of brains and gorgeousness! Was there any explanation?"

"Just the usual — she'd been depressed lately. Dad is over at their house now. Alex called him first, then the police. The medical examiner is there, too."

"Did she OD?"

"She took a bottle of Scotch to the garage and sat in the car with the motor running. I'm due at the hospital now. I'll call you later."

"How about dinner tonight?"

"Sorry, lover. I have to attend a baby shower, but I'll drop in beforehand and you can fortify me with a gin and tonic. I may have more information by then."

When he broke the news to Mrs Cobb, she said, "I feel terrible about it! She was such a lovely person."

Qwilleran said, "Now would be the time for me to type some catalogue cards for you. I'd welcome the distraction."

The task required even more concentration than he expected. First he had to decipher the registrar's notes. Someday he would compose a magazine piece on the subject, titled "How Not to Write Right; or, Seven Easy Ways to Total Obfuscation."

It was like cracking a secret code. As soon as he discovered that a "habimeon glooo luptii" was actually a Bohemian glass luster, the rest was easy. On each card he had to type the file number of the artifact, its name, date, description, provenance, and value. The four-digit and five-digit evaluations kept him in a state of fiscal shock.

Naturally the Siamese were on the desk, assisting in their own unhelpful way. Yum Yum was stealing pencils and pushing paper clips to the floor. Koko, friendly once more after Qwilleran's apology, was nosing about the desktop like a bloodhound. At one point he flushed out Penelope's thank-you note written after the dinner party, and Qwilleran noted her mannered handwriting and the affected *e*, *r* and *s* that somehow implied a classical education.

When Melinda arrived after office hours, she explained, "I'd rather go to dinner with you, lover, but my generation is always getting married or pregnant, and I have to go to cute showers with cute invitations, cute guessing games, cute table decorations, and cute refreshments. When I marry, I'm going to elope. Would you care to elope, lover?"

"Not until they take out my itching stitches. Sit down and tell me how Alexander is reacting."

Melinda curled up in one of the solarium's big wicker chairs. "Dad had to sedate him. Alex got terribly emotional. He and Penny were very close — only a year apart — and they grew up like twins. He feels guilty for spending so much time out of town. He wishes he'd stayed home last night instead of going to a bachelor party at the club. Did you know he's getting married?"

"I heard a rumor."

"She's an attorney — young — graduated top of her class."

"Do you know her name?"

"Ilya Smfska."

Qwilleran nodded. That much checked out; Penelope hadn't been merely garbling her diction. "Who found the body?"

"Alex got home just before daylight, drove into the garage, and there she was."

"Did they establish the time of death?"

"Two a.m."

"Any suicide note?"

"Not as far as I know. Everyone knows she's been overworked, but the ironic fact is that Alex's fiancée could have relieved her caseload. But it's too late now."

She finished her cool drink, declined another, and prepared to leave for her social obligation. "Anyway," she said with a cynical smirk, "Penelope won't have to attend any more showers."

After dinner Qwilleran went for a slow, thoughtful walk down Goodwinter Boulevard. The old family mansion that Penelope and Alexander had shared was partly obscured by twelve-foot hedges, but several cars could be seen in the driveway. Beyond them was the five-car attached garage, obviously a modern addition to the turreted, gabled, verandaed house. Next door was another Goodwinter residence, much less pretentious, where Dr Halifax lived with his invalid wife. It had been Melinda's childhood home.

A raucous blast from a car horn alerted Qwilleran, and he saw Amanda turning into a driveway across the boulevard.

"Come on in for a shot," she called out with gruff heartiness.

"Make it ginger ale, and I'll take two," he said.

The interior of the designer's house appeared to be furnished with clients' rejects. (He wondered if the Hunzinger chair and Pennsylvania *Schrank* had been headed for this eclectic aggregation.) The furniture was cluttered with design magazines, wallpaper books, and fabric samples.

"Move those magazines and sit down," Amanda said. "Had a little excitement in the neighborhood last night."

"Her act was unthinkable!" Qwilleran said.

"Not to me! I knew that unholy situation was headed

for an explosion, but I didn't figure on suicide. I thought she'd blow her brother's brains out, if he has any."

"Do you think it was really suicide?"

Amanda put down her glass on a porcelain elephant table and stared at her visitor. "Golly, that's something I never thought of. Murder, you mean? You can't pin it on Alex. He was at the club all night, playing cards with Fitch and Lanspeak and those other buzzards. Or so the story goes. Now you've got me wondering."

Qwilleran stood up and looked out the front window. "You can see their driveway from here. Did you notice any other vehicle there last night?"

"Can't say that I did. What do you think could have happened?"

"Someone could have drugged her drink and then carried her out to the garage and turned on the ignition, leaving a Scotch bottle for evidence. It's an attached garage. It could be done under cover."

"Say, this is hot stuff!" Amanda said with evident relish. "Wait till I pour another."

"Of course," Qwilleran went on, "the killer would most likely park elsewhere and arrive on foot. Is there any access to the property from the rear?"

"Only through Dr Hal's garden."

"Don't mention this to anyone," Qwilleran requested, "but let me know if you come up with a possible clue."

"Hot damn! Just call me Nora Charles."

Qwilleran walked home slowly, and as he approached the K mansion he saw a terrain vehicle pulling away and heading north.

"Whose truck was that in the drive, Mrs Cobb?"

She was looking radiant. "Herb Hackpole was here. He went fishing this afternoon and brought us a mess of perch, boned and everything."

"You seem to have made a hit with that guy."

"Oh, he's very nice, Mr Q. He wants to take me fishing someday, and he offered me a good trade-in on my van, if I want to switch to a small car. He even wants to take me hunting! Imagine that!"

Qwilleran grumbled something and retired to his Chippendale sitting room, taking a volume of Trollope that Koko had knocked off a library shelf, but even the measured prose of *He Knew He Was Right* could not calm an underlying restlessness. His moustache was sending him signals so violent and so bothersome that he considered shaving it off. Only a critical examination in the bathroom mirror forestalled the rash action.

After a night of fitful sleep he again busied himself with the catalogue cards, but the morning hours dragged by. He glanced at his watch every five minutes.

At long last Mrs Cobb announced a bit of lunch in the kitchen. "Only leftover vichyssoise and a tuna sandwich," she said.

"I can eat anything," Qwilleran told her. "Leftover vichyssoise, leftover Chateaubriand, leftover strawberry shortcake — anything. I wonder how many Castilian monks sat at this table four centuries ago and had broiled open-face tuna sandwiches with Dijon mustard and capers. They're delicious, Mrs Cobb."

"Thank you. How are you getting along with the typing? Are you getting bored?"

"Not at all. It's highly educational. I've just learned that the chest of drawers in the upstairs hall is late baroque in lignum vitae with heartwood oystering. The knowledge will enrich my life immeasurably."

"Oh, Mr Q! You're just being funny."

"Where are the cats? They're suspiciously quiet. Can't they smell tuna?"

"When I called you for lunch, they were both in the vestibule, waiting for the mail."

"Crazy guys!" Qwilleran said. "They know it's not delivered until midafternoon." Yet, he had to admit that he too was waiting for something to happen.

After lunch he returned to his typewriter and was translating "johirgi fiwil hax" into "Fabergé jewel box" when the pitter-patter on the marble floor announced the arrival of the post. An influx of get-well cards was now added to the daily avalanche pouring through the mail slot. Next he heard sounds of swishing, skittering, and scrambling as the Siamese pounced on the pile, sliding and tumbling with joy and talking to themselves in squeaks and mumbles.

Qwilleran let them have their fun. He was busy recording a pair of Hepplewhite knife boxes with silver escutcheons, worth as much as a cabin cruiser, when Koko labored into the library lugging a long envelope in a rich ivory color. Qwilleran knew that stationery, and his moustache sprang to attention. Feverishly he ran a letter knife across the top of the envelope. There were three pages of single-spaced typing on the Goodwinter & Goodwinter letterhead. It was dated two days before, and the signature had the eccentric *e* and *r* that he recognized.

He read the letter and said to himself, She was right; she should have been a writer; she could have written gothic romances.

Dear Qwill,

If I disgraced myself last evening, please be understanding, and I implore you to read this letter with the sympathy and compassion you evinced during my visit.

As I write this I am of sound mind — and perfectly sober, I assure you. I am also bitter and contrite in equal proportions. Obviously I am still among the living, but such will not be the case when you receive this letter. Mrs Fulgrove has instructions to drop it in the mail in the event of my sudden demise. She is the only person I can trust to carry out my wishes. And if I seem calm and businesslike at this moment, it is because I am endeavoring to emulate you. I have, and always have had, a great deal of admiration for you, Qwill.

In writing this painful confession, my only hope is that you are alive to read it. Otherwise a great misfortune will befall the people of Moose County. If I can save your life and prevent this — by accusing certain parties — I shall have done penance for my transgressions.

How does one begin?

I have always loved my brother with an irrational passion. Even as a child I was enamored and possessive, yearning for his attention and flying into a rage if he bestowed it elsewhere. Eventually Alex went away to prep school and I was sent to boarding school, but we were always together weekends.

When my father begged me to study law for Alex's sake, I put aside my ambition to be a writer and attended law school gladly. My grandfather had been a chief justice; my father was a brilliant attorney respected in the entire state. It was intended that Alex should follow in their footsteps. Unfortunately, as my father pointed out, his only son-and-heir would never be more than a third-rate lawyer. I was elected to compensate for his shortcomings and maintain the Goodwinter reputation in the legal field

I never regretted my role, because it meant Alex and I could be together constantly. My rude awakening occurred five years ago when I discovered he was having an affair with our live-in maid. It was a knife in my heart! Not only had he betrayed me, but he had consorted with the commonest of females — a girl from the Mull tribe. I dismissed her at once.

But worse was yet to come. It was the shattering news that she was pregnant and expected to marry her "Sandy," as she impudently called him. After a brief moment of panic, I steeled myself and devised a constructive solution. I would arrange to send her away for an abortion and pay her to relocate in another state.

But no! Her mother, a woman of dubious reputation, influenced her to decline the abortion and file a paternity suit. My God! That such a calamity should happen to our branch of the family! I was infuriated by the arrogance of these people! In desperation I approached one of Alex's boyhood acquaintances and enlisted his cooperation.

Let me explain. When Alex and I were young, Father insisted that we attend public school in Pickax, expecting democratization to shape our life attitudes. On the contrary, we were harassed by the hateful middle-class children. I used my wits to keep them in their place, but Alex was weak and an easy target for their cruelty. I was obliged to go to his rescue.

I hired the school bully — with my own money — to keep Alex's tormentors in line. He continued as bodyguard and avenger until Father saw fit to send us to better schools in the East.

Five years ago — in our new hour of trouble — I begged the same man to convince the Mull girl to submit to an abortion and leave town permanently, in return for a generous financial arrangement, of course. Lest the support payments be traced to their source, it was agreed that cash would regularly be turned over to our intermediary — to be forwarded, less his commission, to the girl. This subterfuge was my idea. How clever I thought I was! Actually, how naive!

At the time of the girl's departure there was a cave-in at Three Pines Mine, on the heels of which that thoroughly amoral and despicable man gloatingly informed us that she was buried a thousand feet underground and would make no more trouble.

He pointed out, however, that we were accomplices before the fact.

The deed was done! No amount of remorse would undo the crime. It remained only to avoid scandal at all costs. The cash payments continued, increasing regularly with inflation and the man's greed. But, at least, Alex and I felt safe, and we had each other.

Then, to my horror, Qwill, you arrived on the scene and raised questions about the missing housemaid — although how your suspicions were prompted, I cannot fathom. It came to our attention that you were talking freely about the matter and interviewing possible witnesses.

The two men agreed between themselves that the two witnesses should be silenced, and I reluctantly agreed. What else could I do? But when they discussed ways to stop your meddling, Qwill, I was appalled! I pointed out that your death would mean the loss of billions of dollars in Moose County. My arguments accounted for nothing. They cared only about saving their own skins.

You have suspected a plot against your life, and you were right to do so. You have misidentified the conspirators, however. Now you know the truth.

For five years I have lived with this specter of guilt and fear. It was bearable only because I had saved the family from unthinkable scandal — and because I had Alex's love.

And then he broke the terrible news that he was bringing a "brilliant" young attorney to Pickax as a partner in the firm and — this was the crushing blow — as a wife!

It was more than I could bear. My lifetime of sacrifice and devotion was thrown aside in a moment. I had involved myself in heinous crime, only to have it end like this — only to be cast aside.

What could I do? There was only one way to stop it. In a frenzy of desperation I confronted Alex and threatened to reveal his complicity in three murders. The instant the words were out of my mouth I realized I had made a fatal mistake. My God! The hatred in my brothers eyes! How can I describe the rage and vengeance that contorted my brother's features — the face that I had thought so beautiful!

Forgive me if I appear melodramatic, but I now fear for my life. I fear that every day may be my last. A bullet from the same rifle that killed the farm girl will be quick and merciful or they will devise a means that will simulate an accident or suicide.

In any event, Mrs Fulgrove will mail this letter, and I am following your example in preparing letters for the prosecutor and the media, naming the brute who killed the pregnant girl, burying her alive in a mineshaft, who arranged a friendly drink with her mother and drugged the whiskey, who fired a single perfect shot at a girl on a farm tractor.

You are not safe, and the future of Moose County is at stake, until these two men are apprehended and brought to justice.

Yours in good faith,
Penelope Goodwinter

CHAPTER SIXTEEN

The shriek of a bomb and the boom of a cannon shattered his frightening dream of global war. He struggled to shake off sleep.

Another boom! Was it a figment of his dream, or was something battering the bedroom door?

Boom! Qwilleran rolled out of bed and groped his way to the door, staggering with sleep. He stopped, listened, reached cautiously for the doorknob. He yanked it open! And a cat hurtled into the room.

Koko had been throwing his weight against the securely latched door, trying to break it down. Now, with stentorian yowls that turned to shrieks, he raced to the staircase.

Qwilleran, not stopping for slippers or robe or light switches, followed as fast as he could while the cat rushed ahead, swooping downstairs, bounding back upstairs to scold vehemently, then flying down again in one liquid movement.

The house was in darkness, save for a dim glow from streetlights on the Circle. Qwilleran moved warily toward the rear of the house where Koko was leading him, now in stealthy silence. Reaching the library, the man heard the back door being unlocked and slowly opened, and he saw a dark bulky figure moving furtively through the entry hall. Qwilleran stepped aside, shielded by the Pennsylvania *Schrank*, while a white blur rose to the top of the seven-foot wardrobe.

Unmindful of the cold stone floor under his feet but thinking wildly of baseball bats and crowbars, Qwilleran watched the intruder pass the broom closet, hesitate at the kitchen door, then enter the large square service hall where the *Schrank* stood guard. There was not a sound. Qwilleran could hear his own heartbeat. Koko was somewhere overhead, crouching between two large, rare, and valuable majolica vases.

As the dark figure edged closer, Qwilleran reached for the toprail of an antique chair, but it was wobbly with age and would shatter if used as a weapon. Just then he heard a barely audible "ik-ik" on top of the *Schrank*, and he remembered the pickax in the library. He slipped into the shadows to grope for it. There were only seconds to spare!

His hand was closing around the sturdy handle when a confusion of sounds broke the silence: a thump, a clatter, a man's outcry, and a loud thud — followed by the unmistakable crash of an enormous ceramic vase on a stone floor. Qwilleran sprang forward with the pickax raised, bellowing threats, towering over the figure that now lay prone.

With squeals and shrieks Mrs Cobb rushed downstairs and the house flooded with light.

"Call the police," Qwilleran shouted, "before I bash his brains!"

The man lay groaning, one arm twisted at a grotesque

angle and one foot in the cats' spilled commode. The shards of majolica were scattered around him, and Koko was sniffing in the pocket of his old army jacket.

"Koko never ceases to amaze me," Qwilleran said to Melinda at the dinner table that evening. "He knew someone was going to break in, and he knew far enough in advance to get upstairs and wake me up. The way he threw himself against my door, it's a wonder he didn't break every bone in his body. The fantastic thing is: he pushed his commode to a spot where the guy was sure to trip over it. The majolica vase is a small price to pay for his heroism."

Qwilleran and Melinda were having dinner at Stephanie's, the Lanspeaks' new restaurant. He called for her at her father's house on Goodwinter Boulevard, where she was changing clothes after a hard day at the clinic, giving allergy shots and bandaging Little Leaguers.

Dr Halifax greeted him at the door. "You had another narrow escape last night, Qwill. You live a charmed life. The needles and morphine they found on him were stolen from my office a short time ago."

"What's his condition?"

"Compound fracture. Dislocated shoulder. He's a heavy fellow, and he went down like a ton of bricks on your stone floor. He's a police prisoner, of course, and a broken arm is the least of his troubles."

Qwilleran and his date walked to the restaurant, which occupied an old stone residence rezoned for commercial use.

"The Lanspeaks named it after their cow," Melinda

said, "and they did the whole place in dairy colors: milk white, straw beige, and butter yellow. It's a service-oriented restaurant."

Qwilleran grunted. "What this town needs is a food-oriented restaurant."

A young hostess greeted them. "My name is Vicki, and I'm your hostperson. Your waitperson is Matthew, and he'll do everything possible to make your visit enjoyable."

A young man immediately appeared. "My name is Matthew. I am your waitperson, and I am at your service."

"My name is Jim," Qwilleran replied. "I am your customer, and I am very hungry. The lady's name is Melinda. She is my guest, and she is hungry, too."

"And thirsty," Melinda added. "Okay, Qwill, tell me all about the break-in last night. How did he get into the house?"

"Birch is pretty crafty. He made an extra key for himself when he installed our new back-door lock. Evidently he waited for a moonless night — there was a heavy cloud cover — and approached through the orchard behind the house. His truck was hidden in the old barn out there. I suspect he was going to haul me away to one of the mine sites and dump me down a shaft."

"Darling, how horrible!"

"I had a look at the truck this morning, and it's the same terrain-buggy that tried to run me down on Ittibittiwassee Road. I recognized the big rusty, grinning grille from my dream. We can also assume it was Birch who doped

Penelope's Scotch and carried her out to the garage while Alex was establishing his alibi at the club."

Matthew arrived with Melinda's champagne and Qwilleran's mineral water. "This is your champagne cooler," he said, "and these are your chilled glasses."

"We'd also like an appetizer," Qwilleran told him. "Bring us some *pâté de caneton.*"

"That's kind of a meatloaf made of ground-up duck," the waitperson explained helpfully.

"Thank you, Matthew. It sounds delicious."

Melinda drank a toast to Qwilleran for exposing a deplorable crime.

Apologetically he said, "I'm afraid it's going to be a nasty scandal when everything comes to light."

"A lot of us guessed the relationship between Penny and Alex," she said, "but who would dream they'd collaborate in a murder plot? And who would ever imagine he'd conspire to kill his sister? He needed her! She was the mainstay of his career."

"Not anymore. He found another brilliant woman — with Washington connections — to take her place. Penelope became a threat. She knew too much, and she was too smart."

Melinda gazed at Qwilleran with admiring green eyes. "No one thought to question Daisy's disappearance before you came here, lover."

"I can't take credit. It was Koko who sniffed out the clues. A couple of days ago he rooted out Penelope's thank-you note on my desk, and I checked it against the postal card from Maryland. She had written it in a disguised hand, but some individual letter formations gave it away. It was probably mailed from a suburb in Washington when Alex was on one of his junkets."

"Poor self-inflated Alex," Melinda said. "I hate to think what a court trial will do to him — his ego, I mean. He was a wreck, Dad told me, after his session with the prosecutor today."

"Birch and Alex may have done the dirty work, but I think Penelope was the mastermind. After I started inquiring about Daisy, Birch started doing a lot of work for us. I thought he was hooked on Mrs Cobb's cooking, but in retrospect I believe Penelope hired him to spy on us. *Someone* was in a position to know I was talking to Tiffany Trotter and was about to talk to Della Mull. They were probably the only two who knew the identity of Daisy's Sandy."

"Didn't you ever suspect Penelope?"

"Well, she changed the subject whenever I mentioned Daisy, but I thought she considered it gauche to discuss servants. I admit I was puzzled when she repeatedly declined my invitations to lunch or whatever."

"No mystery," Melinda said. "I told her to keep hands off or I'd spread some unsavory rumors."

"Melinda, you're a nasty green-eyed monster."

"All Goodwinters have a nasty streak; it's in our genes."

After studying the menu they ordered trout *amandine*.

"That's trout with almonds," said the waitperson, eager to be of service.

"Fine. And we'd like asparagus."

"That's extra," Matthew warned.

While they waited for the entrée Melinda said to

Qwilleran, "So you were wrong about the New Jersey connection. There was no sinister plot to eliminate you and grab the inheritance."

He looked sheepish. "That's what happens when I jump to my own conclusions instead of getting my signals from Koko. You know, that cat is ten pounds of bone and muscle in a fur coat, with whiskers and a long tail and a wet nose, but he's smarter than I am. Without ever visiting Daisy's apartment, *he knew* something was wrong. *He knew* Penelope's final letter was going to be delivered. *He knew* Birch was sneaking up to the house last night."

"Cats have a sixth sense."

"Six! I say Koko has sixteen!"

"If only he could communicate!"

"He communicates all right. The problem is: I'm not smart enough to read him. Let me tell you something, Melinda. When I got the notion that the whole state of New Jersey was after me, Koko was disgusted; he avoided me for days. At one point he pushed some books off a shelf in the library, and I scolded him for it. Do you know what the books were? A poem titled *Doomsday* by a seventeenth-century Scottish poet named *Sir William Alexander*!"

The entrée was served. "This is your trout *amandine* and asparagus on heated plates," said Matthew.

Qwilleran stared at the vegetables. "This isn't asparagus. It's broccoli."

"Sorry. I'll take it back." Matthew removed the plates but soon returned with them. "The chef says it's asparagus."

They ate their trout and broccoli in silence until Qwilleran said, "If Koko hadn't sniffed out the Daisy situation, and if I hadn't started investigating, Penelope and Tiffany and Della would be alive today."

"And a murderer would be at large," Melinda reminded him.

"The Goodwinter reputation would be intact, and Alexander would run for Congress. He'd marry Ilya Smfska and produce another generation of supersnobs."

"And the murderer and his accomplices would live happily ever after."

"Penelope would eventually make an emotional adjustment," Qwilleran said, "and Alexander would keep on paying for Birch Tree's boats and trucks and motorcycles, but he could afford it."

"And no one would care that Daisy was buried in the Three Pines mineshaft," Melinda said.

After the tossed salad on a chilled plate with a chilled fork, and after the Ribier grapes with homemade cheese, and after coffee served with Stephanie's own cream, Qwilleran and Melinda walked back to her father's house.

Dr Halifax met them at the door. "Prepare for some jolting news," he said. "Just heard it on the radio. A private plane crashed fifty miles south of the airport, and the pilot has just been identified."

"Alexander," Qwilleran said quietly, as his moustache bristled.

Back at the mansion he was greeted by a prancing Siamese. Koko knew it was time for the nightly house check, and he led the way to the solarium.

"Case solved," Qwilleran said to him, "but I'd like to know the real reason why you pushed those things around the kitchen. Were you trying to tell me to get that cold stone floor carpeted?"

He finished locking the French doors, and Koko preceded him to the breakfast room. While the man checked the Staffordshire figurines and German regimental steins, the cat checked for stray crumbs under the table.

"Tell me something," Qwilleran said to him. "When you found Daisy's diary, were you just chasing a fly? And if so, how come it happened to be crawling about Sandy Goodwinter's initials?"

Koko bounded ahead to the library, where he pawed a leather-bound copy of *The Physiology of Taste*. In the dining room he sniffed the carved rabbits and pheasants on the sideboard. Then he marched into the drawing room, zigzagging across the Aubusson rug to avoid the roses in the pattern. While Qwilleran gave the bronzes and porcelains a security check, Koko headed for the antique piano.

Leaping lightly to the cushioned bench, he reached up with his right paw in an indecisive way, then withdrew it. After a few tentative passes with his left paw, he planted it firmly on G and then C. He seemed pleased with the sound made by the keys. More confidently he hit the D with his right paw and finally touched the E.

Qwilleran shook his head. "No one would believe it!" He switched off the lights and strode to the kitchen, humming the tune Koko had played: "How Dry I Am!"

Yum Yum was asleep on her blue cushion, and Qwilleran stroked her fur before opening the refrigerator. He splashed a jigger of white grape juice in a saucer, placed it on the floor, and watched Koko lap it up with lightning-fast tongue, his tail curled high in ecstasy.

"I'll never figure you out," Qwilleran said. "You're all cat, and yet you sense the most incredible secrets. You were fascinated by Penelope, and it wasn't just her French perfume. You howled at the exact hour when she died."

Koko licked the saucer dry and started to wash up.

"Did you know she was going to be murdered?"

Koko interrupted his ablutions to give Qwilleran a penetrating stare, and the man slapped his forehead as the truth struck him. "It wasn't a homicide set up to look like a suicide. She framed those guys! It was suicide planned to look like murder!"

Koko finished his chore, with great care to wash behind his ears, between his toes, and all along his whip of a brown tail.